COVETING CHLOE

TRIS WYNTERS

To the woman who just want to be thrown around like a ragdoll.
Enjoy,
XOXO Tris

Contents

Content/Trigger Warnings

Mafia

MMF

Shooting

Bombs

Forced Proximity

Kidnapping

BDSM

Bondage

Squirting

Edging

COVETING CHLOE

1

~Prologue~

A storm rages outside the tiny window of the plane. We're waiting for the "all clear" so we can unload, and get on with our lives. But, I'm perfectly content sitting here, watching the lightning scatter across the sky as the rain trails down the window.

I'm sitting here, completely broken, totally alone. However, the storm reminds me that there'll be sun in the morning.

I hope.

The Captain finally turns off the seat belt sign and I stand to grab my luggage from the overhead bin, then grab my laptop case underneath my seat.

Twenty minutes later, and a whole ass coffee, I find myself at the baggage corral; absent-mindedly watching the bags fly down the slide before being dumped onto the rotating conveyor belt.

It's funny because, at this moment, I kind of relate to the luggage.

I've been shrouded in darkness for so long and now I've been dumped somewhere totally new, totally fresh.

And, it's totally terrifying.

But, it's needed.

I spent four years busting my own ass to get through college with the help of two full-time jobs and a lot of powdered macaroni and cheese. None of my friends really knew how hard I was struggling because, frankly, they didn't need to know.

I thought I had it all. My future was mapped out in front of me. I was going to be a teacher in the same district I was bullied in. And I was going to marry the love of my life, Gage.

But, that all changed last week when I watched him kill a man, slaughtered him in cold blood in the middle of the night while I finished getting my latest tattoo. A tattoo that was supposed to remind me not to let my past swallow my future.

I'll never forget walking out of the shop, searching for him. When he wasn't in the car, I walked around the corner to the nearby custard shop. And, low and behold, there he was, pointing a gun directly between some man's eyes. I didn't even have time to question what I was seeing before the shot echoed down the alleyway. It wasn't as loud as I thought it would be. I don't know, maybe there was a silencer or something, but there was no missing the way the man's body dropped to the ground like a sack of mulch.

I can't lie—I was a coward. Instead of screaming and begging for help, I ran around the corner, back to the black Audi sedan, and slouched against the car until I could control my breathing.

Then, I made a plan.

I whipped out my phone to check my finances, moved everything around as quickly as possible, and then texted him that I was feeling sick and must be coming down with the flu.

He ran back toward the car so fast that I was sure he had caught me snooping around.

But instead, he palmed my forehead, kissed my temple, and lifted me off the ground.

After a stop at the local drugstore, and a ridiculous amount of soup, he put me to bed and walked out of my apartment.

It took me a week to find a teaching gig out of state, pack up my meager contents, and quit my job. Thankfully, I didn't really have any other friends or relationships save for a few people who were more drinking buddies than friends. My mom died a couple of years ago, and my Dad abandoned us before he even knew she was pregnant.

An old friend from high school quickly provided me with a new identity. We swapped my middle name for my first name and gave me a new last name. I am now Grace Espinoza.

Yup, I basically changed nationalities.

I didn't want any ties to my old life, and a basic Italian last name like my given name, Rossi, would be a dead giveaway. Thankfully, I had a decent-sized nest egg that will help me build a new life.

Far, far away.

Gage took up so much of my time that I stopped trying to be anything else with anyone else. His love, his smile, and his presence were an addiction.

One I needed to sober up from immediately; and permanently.

My luggage drops onto the conveyor, and I pick it up before turning around and marching straight to the cab lines.

I hate taxis, but my car broke down a few months ago and is now in a junkyard somewhere. Once the insurance money was paid out, I never bothered shopping for a new one since Gage drove me everywhere.

But, now, I'll definitely need to see the dealer this weekend. Until then, Josef the cabby will have to suffice.

The stench of three-day-old burgers and stale cigarettes causes me to wrinkle my nose as I rest my forehead against the smeared window.

The freeways are different from back home, always bustling with people coming and going. Here, though, only a few cars dot the pavement, seeming to be in no hurry to get anywhere at all.

The highway gives way to a derelict suburban area, where the houses are covered in thick, green vines, and the yards appear to have been forgotten.

Within a few minutes, we're pulling up to a semi-rundown area. It's not awful, but it could definitely use a facelift.

My new apartment is on the fifth floor, and I'm thankful that the elevators work. After a quick stop at the leasing office for the key and to sign last-minute documents, I'm opening the door to a small studio apartment.

A simple kitchen sits to my right, and the small foyer opens to the main living room. To the left is a queen-sized bed, and, down a tiny hall, is the bathroom.

I'm making a list of everything I need when my phone rings. *Crap on a cracker. It's Gage...again.* I send him to voicemail and shoot him a text.

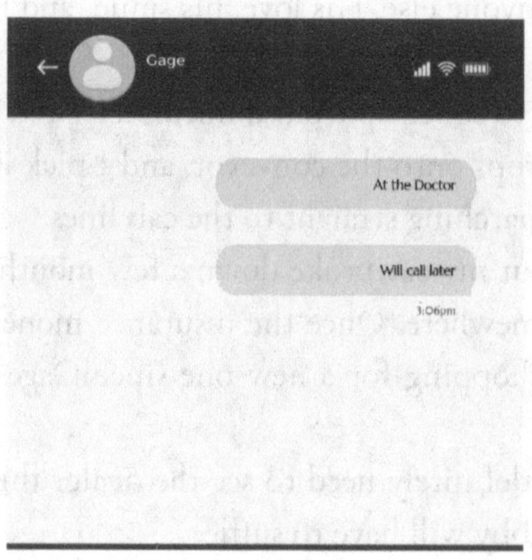

I watch with bated breath as the little blue dots mock me, reminding me of what I left behind. So, I do what any woman on the run would do: turn off my phone and smash it under my heel.

Adding a new phone to my list, I grab my cross-body bag and head out the door.

The good news about my little apartment is that I'm within walking distance of quite a few restaurants, a drugstore, and even a Wal-Mart.

But I can't walk to the school I'll be working at, so the first thing's first…a car.

Thankfully, the storm has passed, so I'm not battling the rain without an umbrella. Instead, I'm playfully jumping in puddles and allowing myself to smile for the first time in a week.

The *thump-thump-thump* of a bass vibrates from the corner of the next street. *Big and Beautiful* is lit up in bright pink neon lights. I smile, excited to find a little bar that at least sounds fun, so close to home.

But first, a car.

Three long, grueling hours later, I'm driving off the lot in a white Honda Civic—a basic car for a basic girl. And, I'm ok with that.

On my way home, though, I remembered the bar around the corner and decided to stop in. Wal-Mart will still be open later, and I could use a drink after dealing with that sweaty salesman, *Steve*.

Finding an open spot near the back, I notice how packed it is for a Thursday—really packed!

Men and women alike flock through the doors dressed in every way possible. Some are clothed in tiny little dresses and heels, some in jeans and nice shirts, some just in cut-off shorts and tank tops.

Either way, this appears to be the place to go around here.

Grabbing my bag, I head to the door, passing the man my new ID. Once he verifies that I'm over 21, I get a glowing smiley face on my hand just as the giant door opens to reveal…

Holy Shit! This place is awesome!

There are dozens of patrons milling about, each with their choice of beverage for the night.

But what grabs my attention is the woman on stage. She's a little bigger than I am, maybe a 20, but she's memorizing the crowd with a firey baton show to the beat of Soap by Melanie Martinez.

She's dressed in skintight leather shorts that stop just below her ass and a black leather bra that crisscrosses in the front, showing off an ample amount of cleavage. Her eyes close as she gets lost in the music, and, for just a moment, I'm jealous of the woman on stage. She's so free, so pure, so...unapologetically her.

"She's pretty wonderful, isn't she?" A high male voice calls out from behind me.

I whirl around to see a man with barely anything but a wide smile. He tilts his head and assesses me for a moment before asking. "Drink?"

I consider it for a second before nodding and giving him my order.

He begins happily chattering away, clearly knowing I'm a newbie. He talks excitedly about the entertainers, how the place will soon open into a club, and everything else in between.

I like him. I think I found my new favorite place, I think to myself as I sip on the fruity concoction.

I take a deep breath and smile for the first time in a week.

Maybe this move won't be so bad...

2

~Chloe~

"Hey, Grace! We need another round, babe."

"You got it, Jo!" I respond cheerfully. I have just enough time to get their drinks before heading backstage to prep. Today marks my three-year anniversary of walking away from my old life and into my new one.

My very hot, freeing, amazing new life!

I took one step into Big and Beautiful and immediately fell in love. It ended up being so much like Sky's the Limit back home and is one of the few reminders of my past life that I allow.

At first, I thought it was a strip club, but it's so much more than that. Plus-sized women from all over our town, and neighboring ones, come here to set their bodies and minds free. Some of us dance and/or burlesque, some sing, some do tricks or other talents, but we all similarly embrace our bodies with little to no clothing on.

I never hated my body, per se, but my thyroid issues, and love of food, meant losing weight and being skinny weren't really options for me. Heck, I work out more with my dance numbers now than I ever have, and I'm still the same size.

Although, my ass and calves look so much hotter now!

Setting the drinks down, Jo slips $20 into my ridiculously short shorts. "Can't wait to see whatcha' got for us tonight, babe." I giggle as he bats his eyes at me, then smacks a kiss on my cheek.

Jo was working the bar the first night I popped in here. He wore nothing but a pair of black sparkly underwear and a black suit vest. His signature eyeliner was caked on, and his cheeks shimmered with the glitter he applied. He served me up a Tequila Sunrise and we talked as I "Ooed" and "Awed" through various sets.

When the performances were finished, they opened up a back section, where a giant dance floor took up the primary space. There, members could continue to drink and dance the night away while performers utilized the various cages, stages, and aerial bands.

Needless to say, I got lost in the tequila, the freedom, and the overall feeling of euphoria. By the time I left, I had accidentally landed a job.

It turned out that Jo was a co-owner and was always scouting new talent. He seemed to like my carefree nature and said my smile would attract people for miles. (Ok, and my size *D* breasts, squishy curves, and sexy calves.)

After the first year of juggling being a teacher by day and working at the club three times a week, I found myself longing to be at the club more.

The rules for patrons are strict, so I don't spend my nights getting groped and prodded. Instead, the ladies and I are respected, revered even. So, I quit my teaching job and now perform at the club five nights a week, making more money than I ever thought possible.

It's been two years since I made the decision and, I'm happy to say, that all of my student loans have been paid off, I'm happier than I've ever been, and I absolutely love my life.

Well, mostly.

Dating is, well, it's hard. One thing Gage totally ruined for me was sex. There was nothing vanilla about him. In fact, he introduced me to

BDSM; and a whole checklist of kinks. Unfortunately, finding a man to do those things, to be ok with them, can be rather difficult.

No, I don't tell them on the first date, or even the second. I wait until the mood seems like it may be headed that way before springing it on them. And, no, I'm not asking someone to practice breath play. That's not something you just pull out of left field. I inquire about low-level kinks like spankings, light bondage, nipple clamps, toy play... You get the point.

And, because of this, I have not had sex in three years. I guess I assumed more men would be ok with light kink but, I was wrong.

So very wrong.

Thankfully, there are flowers, and suckers, and all kinds of rechargeable toys. But, dammit, sometimes a woman just wants to be handled like a ragdoll and be called a "good girl."

Well, this woman does.

Fingers snap in front of my face and I realize I was completely zoned out while dressing. *I suppose I'm glad I at least made it to the dressing room.*

"Earth to Grace. You ok there, girl?" Tiffany asks sweetly, a look of concern jacking up her perfect face.

I chuckle and roll my eyes, trying to shake off the memories of the past. "Yup. Just got a little lost in my head. It's scary in there," I joke freely.

She studies me for a moment, squinting just a little. Eventually, she appears to accept my answer. "Ok then, you're on in three. Chop, chop."

I nod and finish changing, fluffing my hair and applying even more glitter to my now mostly naked chest, arms, and belly.

The curtain falls as Sylvie finishes her latest number and she quickly scoops up the cash that was thrown her way.

"Damn girl, you're going to need a bigger wallet." I jest with a smile.

Her brilliant, perfect smile flashes brightly as she nods. "I know, right? They really seem to like the new number. I was worried about belly dancing but, it appears to have been the right change." She says, fanning herself with all the cash.

"Of course it was! It's hot!!"

She rushes off, waving me on as Carrie and Alex take their spots next to me.

The MC announces my name, the curtains go up, and the spotlights sizzle against my nearly-naked flesh as the music begins.

The opening instruments for Looking at Me by Sabrina Carpenter begin to play and my smile goes wide.

Show time.

3

~Mason~

Some snappy little song comes on as I swipe my beer from the table and take a long pull. I'm not paying attention to half the things Marco is saying because I just need to close this deal and get the hell out of here.

The only good thing about this place is the view. Who knew that there was a club for plus-size entertainers? Sure as hell not me, but damn, do I like it.

I always like my women with something to hold on to, something to squeeze, something to...

I choke on my beer, spluttering like a fool when I peer over at the stage, sitting off to my right. A bombshell of a woman is swinging her hips to the beat of a song I could care less about.

Except, I do... I do care about it because she matches each sensual chord with a sway of her hips; her belly and white, sparkling lingerie-covered breasts jiggle perfectly in time with her movements, and, *oh my God! Hot pockets!!!* Deliciously perfect hot pockets on each of her inner thighs.

Shoot me; I must be dreaming.

The woman's bright blue eyes hold me hostage as her wavy, chocolate locks spin around with her twirl. She bends down and pops her luscious ass out, and I almost cream my pants like a horny teenager.

She's wearing barely-there white, sparkling booty shorts that match her bra. Her ass isn't big like a bubble, it's big like a platter. Two perfect globes large enough to hold a full fucking handprint.

Yup, I must be dead. Because this is heaven, and she's an angel.

Someone nudges me, and I quickly turn to find Marco grinning at me like a smug bastard. Rolling my eyes, I clear my throat and take another long pull from my beer. "Sorry, what were you saying?"

Marco and his guys laugh out, briefly making me feel like an idiot. But I can't help it. Just look at her... "I said, she's a nice piece of ass, no?"

Marco's words have me furrowing my brow in disdain. *How dare he talk about her like that.*

I feel a sneer growing on my face before I realize what I'm even doing.

I don't even know this woman. *No, but you want to...*

I chastise my inner voice, knowing damn well I'm not here to get laid.

One business deal, close, and home by tomorrow night. *Right.*

Clearing my throat, I redirect our conversation, "So, do we have a deal? 100K up front, then 200K when it's done?"

My mask of indifference slips into place as Marco's falls. I can tell he's thinking it over, trying to figure out a negotiation. But he doesn't know me. No one out-negotiates me.

"150K up front." He replies with a sly smirk.

I stare at him, unblinking. I wait until his smirk begins to falter, and then I reach my hand out to shake. "Deal."

Dumbass. Of course, we'll give half now and half later. I just didn't want him to know that. Only those we implicitly trust get more.

After shaking, I stand up and button up my suit jacket. With a nod to each man, I smooth down my jacket and curtly end the meeting. "Gentlemen. It was good doing business with you."

Downing the rest of my beer, I drop a hundred-dollar bill on the table, walk over to the stage, and catch the eye of the angel performing.

She grins at me but continues her number, smiling wider as my clear distaste for her ignoring my silent request to come closer becomes evident on my face.

I wait all of ten seconds before whipping my hand out, pulling her down to me, and stuffing a wad of cash into her glittering bra.

Her eyes are wide with fear and...arousal? *No way. I must be seeing things.*

Just as I'm about to let her go, I reach into my pocket and pull out my card, shoving it into the front of her booty shorts.

By the time the owner walks up with a bouncer, I've let her go, spun on my heel, and thrown out another wad of cash.

"Sorry about that," I toss behind me as I walk out the front door.

The humidity in this place is shit, but a cool breeze flips through the air, ruffling a group of leaves nearby.

I head over to my rental car: a Kemora Gray Metallic Audi R8. *Damn, I love this car.*

I hit the radio, buckle up, then speed out of the parking lot. As Play with Fire by Sam Tinnesz filters through the car, I shift and push the pedal to the floor driving further away from the club.

And further away from the angel that I know will plague my mind.

It's only a five-minute drive to the hotel that I'm staying at for the night.

When I pull up, I step out, and hand the valet my keys before swaggering through the automatic door.

I take out my phone and hit the first contact on my Favorites list.

"Mason," I swear his silky voice vibrates through the phone as I step into the elevator alone.

"Boss," I coo seductively.

But, he ignores it, for now. "Is it done?"

"Of course it is. Got 'em for less than we were willing to pay up-front. Stupid fucks." I chuckle and hear him sigh with relief on the other end.

"Good, good. Any plans for tonight?" His tone changes, just barely, and I smirk, knowing exactly what to say to rile him up.

"Not yet. Slipped a sexy little something my number while I was out. We'll see." I play it off like it's no big deal but, I can almost guarantee his reaction.

"Tape it. I want to see every curve, hear every moan. But, most of all, I want to see you get off, knowing that you'll be punished once you come back home."

My cock thickens in my pants and I readjust it as the elevator doors open to my floor.

"Yes, Boss." I swallow audibly, now picturing him jerking himself to a video I make for him.

"Good. And, Mason?"

"Yes?" I respond hesitantly.

"Don't forget who you belong to." He states firmly before disconnecting the call.

Moody bastard.

As much as he loves being with me and controlling me, he loves having a woman involved even more. But he never touches them. He dominates me and commands us both but refuses to cross any other lines.

Not since *her.*

The door dings and the light turns green so I push down the handle and walk into my room. Tearing off my jacket, my tie, and then my shoes, I fling myself onto the bed and flip through the food app to get something delivered.

Maybe I'll hear from a certain angel tonight.

I wonder what she would want to snack on after I snack on her?

4

~Chloe~

"Can you believe the audacity of that man?" Alex asks, flipping her long, red hair over her shoulder.

"Did you see him, Alex? He was the epitome of tall, dark, and delicious." Carrie chides. "I mean, sure, he was probably about to get kicked out, but, damn, girl! I'd have given my left tit for him to manhandle me like that."

I'm only partially paying attention as I cover my white, sparkling bra with a black fishnet shirt.

Since I was barefoot for the performance, I quickly slid into my pink, slip-on Chucks and fluffed my hair back out.

Then and only then do I pull out the obscene wad of cash he stuffed into my bra.

"Holy fuck, girl!" Alex exclaims.

"Jesus! That's gotta be at least $500!" My mouth drops in awe, and a light blush creeps up on my cheeks.

Shifting around, I'm suddenly prodded by the corner of something in my shorts. "What the..." I trail off, reaching in to pluck out a black embossed card.

Alex shrieks indignantly while Carrie's eyes widen in shock. "He gave you his number?"

I try to laugh it off. I mean, does he think I'm a sex worker or something? Does he expect me to give him a happy ending just because he paid me more in one performance than I usually make in a night? *Well, if that's what you want, you've got another thing comin', buddy.*

I slam open my locker and shove the money into my wallet. Then, I pull out my phone.

My mouth opens and closes like I'm a floundering fish. *He can't be serious, right?*

"What did he say?" Carrie implores excitedly, her smile as wide as her face.

"He, um, he wants to see me..." I chew my lip and debate my own sanity. I mean, it's obviously a one-night stand kind of deal, and it has been a while...

"Girl, yes!!! You said you needed to get out more. You know you need this! You deserve this! One night with that delicious morsel of a man. I mean, what could go wrong?" Carrie insists wildly.

I spend the rest of my shift clearing tables and debating whether or not I should respond.

His deep, brown hair fell in loose curls around his face, framing his hazel eyes just perfectly. He screamed *golden retriever with a dark side*; sex, money...and danger.

Of course, it's the danger part that I'm not so sure of. But how dangerous can one night be?

By the end of my shift at 12:30, I'm sincerely debating texting him back. I mean, worst comes to worst, it doesn't happen, or he's fallen asleep. But something tells me he's a night owl through and through.

As I hit the front door and step into the parking lot, I'm struck with a sudden sense of being watched. My spine tingles, and the hair on the back of my neck stand up.

I hurry over to my car, climb in, and then lock the door, frantically searching the lot for anyone who may have been watching.

After a couple of minutes, my heart rate decreases and I've finally convinced myself that I'm being unnecessarily jumpy.

Pulling out my phone, I see that he has texted me twice since our last exchange.

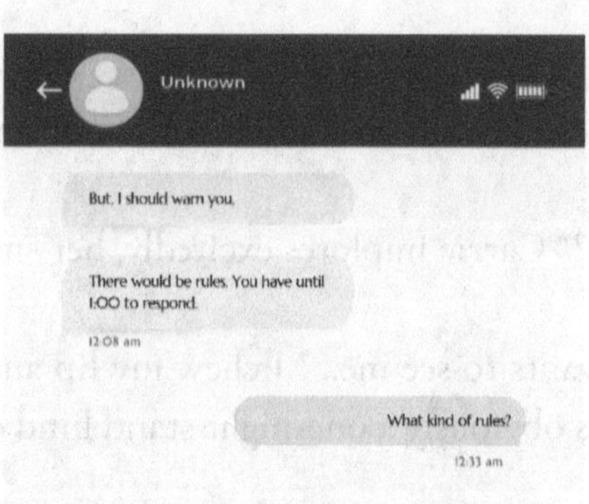

I can't be seriously considering this, right?
Maybe...Maybe not.

Ok, fine, definitely, maybe.

It takes him all of a minute to respond with an address, and my eyes widen as I look it up. It's a fancy, schmancy hotel on the nicer side of town. Like, the kind of hotel that has valets and stuff.

I debate long and hard.

If I'm at a hotel, there will be other people around. Other people to hear me scream if he's really an ax murderer trying to kill me.

Even with that errant thought, something tells me this man may just be the answer to all of my sexual woes. Who knows, maybe I'll finally have found a real Dom in this town. And maybe, just maybe, I'll finally get over my ex.

It takes me thirty minutes to get changed at my apartment and head back out. I definitely wasn't walking through the doors of this hotel looking like a cheap hooker. Nope, not this girl.

I may not be ashamed of what I do for a living, but that doesn't mean I don't follow societal rules about appropriate attire in other places. And this place screams money.

I settled on a lavender blouse that works perfectly with my skin-tight black, ripped jeans and my black wedge sandals. *Cute and classy, just like I am.*

I laugh, knowing damn well I'm not classy, but, hey, tomato, to-mah-toe. Walking through the giant glass door at this hotel, I feel very *un-classy.*

As I head to the elevator, I begin to second-guess this whole decision. *I mean, what the actual fuck am I doing right now? Meeting some random stranger for a booty call? Who am I?*

The golden doors whirr open, and I step inside, trying to calm my frayed nerves. Clicking on the little, round button with the 8 on it, I lean back and breathe deeply while counting to 10. By the time I'm finished, the elevator dings and opens wide to an opulent hallway.

Yes, hallways can be opulent.

The maroon swirls across the light cream carpet match the maroon light shades spaced out on the walls. The walls are creamy and calming, and the door handles are a deep, brassy color.

It really is beautiful.

Once I come to room 818, I pause, my knuckles frozen-mid air, and second-guess whether or not I'm really going to knock; whether I'm really going to do this with a total stranger.

5

~Mason~

I've been pacing the room for what feels like all night, but it's probably just an hour. I can't believe she actually contacted me. I mean, surely she has options, right? And me? Who am I? I don't do one-nighters. Not alone anyway.

With a deep breath, I blow out a raspberry and chuckle to myself. *I'm being ridiculous. She's just a woman, and I'm just a man. We both have needs, and that's what tonight's about. Right? Right.*

The faintest of knocks has me damn near tripping over my suitcase to get to the door. There's a strong possibility I'm going to lose my shit, and not in a fun way.

As I get to the door, I smooth my hands through my curly hair and check to make sure my sleeves are rolled up perfectly, and my shirt's top three buttons are undone. Yes, it's a little weird, but this is how I was taught, and it hasn't let me down yet.

Another faint knock sounds through the door, and I grin. *Clearly, someone is as anxious as I am.*

Blowing out another deep breath, I unlatch the door and pop the lock. I dig deep, summoning my best "Boss Man" energy, then open the door wide. With a smug grin, I greet my angel with a wink. "Glad you could make it. Would you like to come in?"

Her bright, ocean-blue eyes are wide and filled with a healthy dose of fear and arousal.

"Y-yes," She stammers as she pointedly looks anywhere but my face and steps across the threshold.

Once she's far enough in, I close the door, lock it, then latch the emergency lock. *Now she's mine.*

"Would you like something to eat? Drink? I, um-" I'm cut off when she turns those bright eyes on me that seem to peer into my soul.

Her sweet, tinkling giggle carries through the room, and I blink back to my body. *Holy shit, this woman is bad news. Not that it's going to stop me.*

Suddenly remembering my manners, I stick out my hand, like a fucking goober, and say, "I'm Mason." Her eyes sparkle with amusement, and her lips quirk up in a grin.

"Hi, Mason," She chuckles, lightly taking my hand in hers. With a mischievous grin, she follows up with, "Angel is fine for tonight."

With a smile, I brush past her and head for the small bar on the opposite side of the room. Opening it up, I take out a few small bottles of rum, vodka, and tequila. Turning to her, I smile wide and hold up the bottles. "So, what's your poison?" I ask, waggling my brows.

She hums thoughtfully as she steps toward me and slips a bottle of tequila from between my fingers. Hers brush over mine, and my cock hardens with the electricity that sparks between us.

She quickly steps back, runs her hand through her hair, and quickly twists the bottle cap. Not even ten seconds later, she's already downed the whole tiny bottle and then tossed it in the trash. She turns toward me, inhales sharply as she presses her lips together, and lets them go with a loud *smack.*

"Rules." She states firmly.

My brows form a deep v as I frown at her in question. "Rules?" I squeak out, choking on a swallow of rum.

"You said there are rules. So, let's hear 'em." She sits demurely on the edge of the bed, crossing those delicious legs and resting her hands on top of them.

"So, rules." She waves her hand out toward me, quietly insisting that I move on.

"Oh, ok. Yes, um, rules." I swallow the rest of the sweet liquid in the tiny white bottle, then toss it on the bar and face her. I channel my inner Dom and shove my hands in my pockets, relaxing my shoulders and glaring down at her.

I don't miss the way her eyes travel along the veins in my forearms or the way she bites her bottom lip as her eyes dilate with need.

A smirk grows on my face, knowing exactly the kind of sub my little angel is going to be.

"Rules, Angel." I snap, forcing her eyes back to mine.

Her body immediately reacts, just as I hoped. Her eyes dilate, her lids droop a little, and her mouth parts slightly on a pant. "Rule one: I'm in charge. No topping from the bottom, or there will be punishment. Do you know what a safeword is?" I inquire.

She nods her head excitedly and I see a small smile form on her face. "Yes, sir." She bats her eyes.

"But," she begins nervously. "Before we go down that rabbit hole, I want to know what you know and how you plan to proceed."

I tilt my head at her, assessing her response. She's clearly had some issues with fake Doms in the past. With a deep, cleansing breath, I take a step toward her and kneel at her feet. Talking just above a whisper, I say, "As a Dom, it is my job to ensure that you not only enjoy our time together but that you feel safe exploring your kinks with me. Safeword means "stop." Period. And, if there's something we need to adjust, just say "yellow," and we'll make adjustments. Anything else?"

At some point, my hands made their way to hers and are now wrapped around them. Her hands are so small and delicate, and, at this moment, with her eyes sparkling up at me, I'm feeling way more than I should. *Hope.*

She swallows hard, and a grin tips her mouth as she leans down until we're face-to-face. Her breath is warm and minty as she whispers, "Yes. Sir."

A growl rumbles through my chest at the name, and I stand up and tower over her.

"What's your safeword, Angel?" My voice comes out hoarse as my cock hardens almost uncomfortably.

Her eyes widen, and a little tremble moves through her body. "Pink Unicorn," she squeaks out.

My grin turns feral as her head immediately bows toward the floor like the perfect, little submissive.

Fuck this is going to be fun.

6

~Chloe~

Mason is the Dom I've needed for the last three years. My panties are completely soaked, and the man hasn't even touched me yet. There's actually a high possibility that I'm going to die if he doesn't rectify that in the next thirty seconds.

Alas, like a real Dom, he doesn't rush anything. Instead, with my head bowed, staring at the floor, his sexy bare feet come into view. His black slacks brush the tops, and I can't help but wonder if I prefer them on…or off.

Time silently ticks by. My heart rate is galloping loudly, and I swear he can hear it.

"Blindfold?" his smooth, silky voice trails along my cheeks, and they flame in response.

"Y-yes," I respond timidly. Sub-space hasn't even settled in yet, but my anxiety and eagerness are causing my body to riot with fresh tingles of awareness.

A silky tie suddenly hangs in front of my face, just the wide tip coming into view, moments before the smooth, cool fabric is wrapped around my eyes and tightly knotted behind me.

"Good?" He inquires, softly stroking a finger down my puffy cheek.

"Y-yes." I squeeze my thighs together, my heart beating directly in my core as desire floods my system.

"Good girl," he groans while fingering the top of my blouse. "Stand."

On shaky knees, I move to stand. My whole body brushes up against him, but he doesn't move a single muscle out of my way.

By the time I'm standing, my whole body is trembling, and my head is already feeling floaty.

Suddenly, a coolness wafts past my body, and his warmth is noticeably missing. My fear rises up a little higher as I desperately try to hear anything above the sound of my own blood pumping in my ears.

"Strip." His single command causes me to jump. I hadn't anticipated him to be so far away- over by the bar area, presumably in the chair.

With shaky hands, I peel off my top. "Stop!" He barks. "Slower. We have all night."

I swallow past the lump in my throat as I gingerly peel my black lace bra away from my body, pointedly dropping it on the floor near his feet; I hope.

His chuckle sends pulses through my clit, and my panties flood with my arousal.

My fingers tremble as I unbutton, then unzip, my pants and wiggle them down my curves, bringing my panties down with them.

A loud smack, followed by a burst of pain across my left ass cheek, sounds out through the room, and I yelp. "You loopholed, Angel. You know better."

Jesus, how did he move so fast and so quietly?

"S-s-sorry." He's right. I got impatient and took off both articles at the same time.

Standing up taller, he gently rubs a warm, calloused hand over the welp, which I'm sure is forming now.

Then, I hear a ruffle of clothing near my calves and feel his fingers delicately unstrapping my wedged sandal. He slips one off and gracefully moves on to the other.

Once he's finished, he pats my ass and says, "Crawl on the bed, Angel. Let me see my mark."

Embarrassingly enough, I turn and start to climb onto the bed, forgetting that my stupid jeans are still around my ankles. Instead of sexily crawling on the bed- like I wanted- I get caught up, slip, and fall face-first onto the bed.

I'm not sure if I should laugh or cry, so I do neither. Instead, I shimmy my ass up on the bed, putting a little extra into my sway to try and balance out the goofy fall.

But I do feel a couple of runaway tears slip into the tie around my eyes. Thankfully, he doesn't seem to notice as he says, "That's my girl. Oh my God! You should see yourself. Your beautiful, creamy skin wearing my bright, red mark. Mmmm. You look good...enough...to..."

His voice dips lower and lower before trailing off completely.

And then, two fingers suddenly hit my clit, and he immediately swipes them straight up to my ass. I squeal and lunge forward, but his strong, steady hands whip out and steady me. "No. Stay still. You can take it."

My body trembles with his command and the vulnerability I currently feel having my giant ass on display for this man.

His fingers begin swiping through my folds, gathering up my arousal. My breathing is erratic, and I already feel like I'm going to fall face-first into the mattress.

A warm, wet tongue meets my clit, and I mewl in response as his fingers begin to prod my anus. I tense up, unwilling to call my safeword, but never having done *that* before.

"Are you an anal virgin, my Angel?" He inquires, And I swear I can hear the smirk in his voice.

"Uh-um. No, but yes." I don't know why I fear his response, but I do. There's just something about this man that calls to me. That makes me want to tell him things. Even if for a night.

"N-no cock. Only fingers."

He groans long and low, then immediately dives right back in with his tongue, attacking my clit with fervor.

"Dirty words from a dirty girl." He states between flicks and prods of his tongue.

Then, it's like a switch flips. He shoves one long, thick finger deep inside my core, and I groan at the beautiful intrusion. I can feel my eyes roll in the back of my head as his hair tickles the back of my thighs and his tongue skates in figures across my clit.

After a few more fucks of his fingers, he turns them and hits a spot deep inside of me that has me crying out his name.

"Now, come for me, dirty girl." With that, he shoves two fingers into my pussy, his tongue into my ass, and rubs my clit with two gloriously fast-paced fingers. *Holy fork shit!*

I feel him everywhere, and just when I think I can't handle it any longer, he pinches my clit, and I orgasm harder than I have in a very long time. Maybe even in my life.

And that was just the beginning.

As soon as my orgasm crests, I do, in fact, land face-first into the mattress.

The smug bastard chuckles behind me. I don't even have a chance to take another breath when I'm unceremoniously flipped over by my ankles. A squeal slips out of my mouth as his hands press on my thighs, and he opens me wide for him.

Then, his tongue attacks my clit again, causing me to arch off the bed.

"Holy- Oh! Oh! Oh God!"

"Sorry, Angel. There's no God here." With that, he screws two fingers inside of me, pumping them in and out of my clenching pussy at an impossibly fast pace.

His rough, jerking movements bring me to the brink of another orgasm faster than I would have ever guessed.

And then, he stops. His body disappears from between my legs, and I whimper at the loss.

For an eternity, there appears to be no movement, no sound other than my harsh pants filling the space.

My ears strain as I try to track his movements, try to hear where he is, what he's doing, or what he could possibly be thinking. *Did he leave?*

When the silence gets to be far too much, I move to close my trembling legs.

A hard smack lands on my exposed pussy, and I yelp out at the pain and the jarring realization that he's so close.

"Ah, ah, ah," he chastises. "No moving, Angel. I'm admiring what's now mine."

"Y-yours?" I stutter out. I'm not sure about all that, but if he plays his cards right, I could be his for a night.

"Yes, Angel. All mine. Now, legs wide, hands above your head; hold on to the bars of the headboard."

I immediately move to obey, getting in a comfortable position as I hear clothing begin to shuffle. The metal clink of a belt buckle rings out through the room and my core throbs with need.

A sharp slap to my pussy is quickly followed by two more, and I yelp out and moan at the feeling of his fingers softly rubbing circles on my clit.

Finally, the bed between my legs dips. I'm soaking wet, damn near dripping on the sheets, as his body hovers over mine.

"Please," I whine.

"Since you asked so nicely..." His fingers prod my opening, slowly dipping in and out at a leisurely pace. My hips buck at the attention, but his meaty paw presses my pelvis down, forcing my ass to stay on the bed.

"No moving, Angel..." He grits out as he continues his ministrations. "Condom?"

I shake my head back and forth vigorously, not wanting to waste any more time. "Pill. No intercourse in three years. I'm clean. Plleassee!!" I ramble out, trying to buck my hips even though his hold is stable and unmoving.

"Ok, Angel, I've got you." His fingers disappear seconds before the tip of his raging, hard cock.

"Have you ever taken a pierced cock?" He grinds through his teeth.

My mind flashes to images of Gage with his Jacob's ladder of pure pleasure. Is that what this guy has, too?

A sharp sting on my pussy forces me back to the present, and I nod my head.

It only takes me two seconds until I remember to answer... "Y-yes. A long time ago. Jacob's Ladder." I'm delirious with lust and pleasure and, apparently, can't complete full sentences.

"Good. Good girl." His breathing stutters as his tip presses into my core, just past the rim. Something cool and hard causes me to gasp out.

Before I can comment, though, he withdraws a little, and I moan low and long.

My nails scrape against the headboard railings as my pussy fights to keep him inside. Thankfully, he puts me out of my misery as he thrusts in a little deeper. I cry out as the stretch burns and dances with ripples of pleasure.

A slap to my left tit makes me squeal, and he simultaneously rams another couple of inches of his fat cock deep into my quivering pussy. My legs tremble, my arms quake, and a low groan forces its way out of my throat.

"Oh God!"

"No God here," he pants out between breaths. "Just a demon claiming your tight, little, cunt."

We both scream out with pleasure as he slides his big cock out of my clenching pussy and rams all the way in; his balls slapping me against my ass.

We both freeze: me from getting used to his size and him...well, I don't know why.

Then, his warm, soft lips are on mine; sweet, almost loving, tender even. His tongue swipes out against my bottom lip, requesting entrance with a gentle nip. And, I acquiesce to his silent request. My mouth falls open on a gasping moan as he rotates his hips, and I feel his piercing deep inside of me.

He takes the opening and thrusts his tongue into my mouth, lapping at my own with gentle strokes. I'm so lost in the feeling, in the tenderness, that I almost forget that there's a giant dick rammed inside of me.

But then, he withdraws, all the way until the biting metal of his piercing catches on my entrance, just to slam back in again... and again... and again.

Thrust, thrust, thrust.

Our tongues tangle as he begins to pound into me, turning the kiss from sweet and eerily intimate to rushed, passionate, ravaging.

A calloused hand finds my breast and begins to massage it roughly as he thrusts deep inside of me. The massage quickly turns into hissing pain as he tweaks and twists my nipples.

"Fuck! Fuck!" I break the kiss, and my back bows, trying to get away from the pain but also thrusting my tits closer to it. The edge of pleasure and pain is so ridged and narrow that it quickly becomes intoxicating.

After a few more tweaks, he smacks my tit, and I cry out just as he reaches between us and pinches my clit.

I scream toward the ceiling as my orgasm rips through my body and rushes out of my pussy. Somewhere in my subconscious, I can feel him continue to ravage my clit as he brutally fucks me, pushing the last few waves of my orgasm out and causing me to clench around him painfully.

"Goddamn, Angel. That's it. That's my little cock slut."

A trembling groan rumbles through me just as he slips out of my pussy, and flips me over like I'm some tiny thing. My hands quickly find their way to the headboard railing, just in time for him to plunge deep inside of me once more. We both scream out to the heavens as he destroys me: body, mind, and soul.

"Oh God! Please! Oh, oh, God!" I pant nonsensically.

"I already told you, Angel." He growls. "There is no God here. Now, say my name while you milk my cock dry. Give me another."

I shake my head vigorously in protest. "I, I can't." I grit out, my body far too exhausted to perform like someone's little puppet.

Or so I thought.

He growls out, wraps my hair around his hand, and yanks my head back. "One more. Now, cum!" He orders as his free hand ripples over my clit like a trigger-happy fool.

And, damn, I do. I cum so hard that stars spark behind the blindfold, my body tightens like a snake ready to strike, and then...and then...and then...

He rips his throbbing cock from my pussy and continues his assault on my clit until the coil snaps.

My whole body shakes violently as roll, after roll, after roll of my orgasm runs through me. I vaguely feel the bed under my knees turn wet, but my brain isn't functioning enough for me to care.

The moment my orgasm is just about finished, he rams his dick back inside of me once, twice more. Then, he goes rigid and roars out his own release. I feel his cum splashing deep inside of me as my body continues to shake and clench around him.

Eventually, we both fall in a heap on the bed, satiated and perfectly spent.

After a couple of minutes, he gingerly takes the tie away from my eyes. I blink away the first rays of bright light and try to re-center myself. Then, I see his beautiful face and gasp. His golden hazel eyes are so deep, so expressive, so intimate that I have to close my eyes to hide away from the intense feelings that are welling up inside of me.

I take a deep breath and start to sit up, knowing our time together is over. "Hold up, Angel. Let me get the bath."

"Bath?" I squeak in surprise.

His sweet chuckle relaxes me, just a smidge, as he scoots off the bed, his tattooed body rippling with the movement.

And good God!

I ogle that naked, chiseled ass every step he takes to the bathroom. How the hell did I score *that?* Don't get me wrong, I'm a decent girl to look at but holy hotcakes. That man could battle with Gage in the looks department.

Where Gage had deep, dark brown hair, like the sweetest molasses, Mason has rich, chocolatey hair. Gage keeps his floppy on top and shaves close around the sides, while Mason has the most beautiful curls framing his face, trickling to the middle of his neck at the back. And Gage had the deepest, almost steely blue eyes I had ever seen, while Mason has golden-hued, hazel eyes that sparkle with a mixture of playfulness and something... something much darker.

Both men clearly have an affinity for the five-o'clock shadow look, but Mason's wide face opens his angular jawling more than Gage's sharp jawline.

And what is with me and guys with dimples? Mason's dimples could melt butter. But, Gage's dimple in his chin makes you want to say, "Yes, sir" no matter what he's requesting.

Jesus, Chloe. Get a grip! The whole reason you came here was to get over Gage. Do not compare him to your one-night stand.

Thankfully, Mason and his lean, toned body comes stalking out of the bathroom with the tell-tale sounds of the tub filling.

"Alright, Angel. Up you go." He murmurs. At the same time, he lifts me clear off the bed. I squeak with indignation and try to wriggle from his grasp.

"Dude! I'm way too heavy." I giggle out.

A sharp *thwap* to my thigh has my eyes widening like saucers and my arms tightening around his neck, hoping he doesn't drop me on my ass.

"Hush, you aren't too heavy. You're fucking perfect, Angel."

I scoff and roll my eyes. "I didn't say I wasn't perfect. I am what and who I am, and could care less what others think. However, I'd prefer not to have to call the ambulance because you're overzealous ass gets hurt trying to act all chivalrous."

He cackles out. Then, in a move I can't quite comprehend, he shifts me at the same time he steps into the bath, bringing my back to his front while still cradling my legs. Due to the shift, I have to let go of his neck and end up digging my nails into his arms as panic over him dropping me shoots through my body.

"I've got you, Angel." He whispers in my ear as he begins to slowly lower into the most heavenly-smelling bath I've ever been near. The heat causes me to hiss on contact as my sweaty skin hits the water.

After just a short minute, he's fully seated, leaning back against the tub, his arms now banded loosely around my body. I sigh as the heat and Epsom salts soak deep into my muscles and lean my head back against his shoulder.

His contented sigh causes my now-closed eyes to pop open in alarm. He must feel my sudden rigidity as he sweetly coos in my ear while running his large, coarse hands up and down my arms. "Just tonight, Angel. Give me this tonight," He murmurs, leaning his head against mine while continuing to rub my arms lazily.

I exhale in agreement, closing my eyes once more, and allow myself to enjoy this little piece of connection, this little piece of intimacy, *just for tonight.*

7

~Mason~

I wake up the next morning with nothing more than a memory and her sweet scent lingering on the sheets. With a groan, I roll over to find the bed as empty as I knew it would be and a little white paper sitting under the alarm clock. The alarm clock that's blaring a bright red 9:38 am. *Oh crap! I'm late. I never sleep in.*

I swipe the note and hurry over to my suitcase, ripping it open and tugging out a top and some jeans. Thankfully, I had that bath with...with...*Angel* last night, so I'm at least clean. But, damn, I wish I had more time with her.

Or at least knew her name.

I mean, I know we decided on that beforehand, but, shit, one night was *not* enough.

With an aggravated sigh, I dress quickly, ram the note in my pocket, re-zip my suitcase, and head out.

After I step out of the elevator in the lobby, I stroll past the concierge, tipping my head in thanks, and head out the door. Thankfully, my driver is a stupidly patient man and is still at the curb.

Ripping the backdoor open, I shove my suitcase in, slide in behind it, and slam the door. "Sorry. I forgot the alarm."

"It's ok, sir. I already called the jet. They're still on standby."

I double-pat his shoulder and pull my phone out. After shooting off a quick text, I close my eyes and let my head fall back against the seat. Then it hits me...

My eyes spring open as I dig into my other pocket, clasping onto the little white piece of paper.

The only thing I have left of her.

Unfolding the note, I skim the written words, her words, and find myself smiling like a buffoon. Unfortunately, we only got one night, but she did leave a little part of herself. And for that, I will always be grateful.

Damn, I wish I could see her again. And this note makes that feeling deep in my chest ache in the best and worst ways.

Dear Mason,

Thank you for the most amazing night I've had in years. I figured you wouldn't want to do the awkward morning thing so I decided to let you sleep. Besides, I have a shift tomorrow and need to practice.

Good luck with your business deal.

—Angel

Three hours later, I'm stepping onto the tarmac and eye the Z71 Suburban waiting for me. *Guess he's a little pissy that I'm forty minutes late and has decided to punish me sooner rather than later.*

I roll my eyes and begin walking toward the SUV. Just as I approach, the driver steps out, suited out like he's part of the MIB, and opens the back passenger side; a silent command to get in the back.

With a shrug, I slide onto the leather seat and get situated, pointedly *not* looking over at the pissy boss man.

By the time my luggage is in the back, my door is closed, and he gets in the car, I know that I've worn out the procrastination timer.

I lean back and put on my best, lazy grin as I look over at the man sitting in the seat by the other far window and bumble out, "What's up."

His eyes turn hard, angry. He tilts his head and assesses me closer. My hands start to sweat as his eyes bore into mine and I know he can see everything. *Jackass knows me far too well.*

With an audible gulp, I toss out, "Sorry I was late. I forgot to set the alarm."

His brows furrow, a deep v forming between them, and his lips part slightly. "Oh, for fuck's sake!" He scoffs aloud. "She was just a pussy, man. What the hell is wrong with you? Get your fuckin' head in the game."

He shakes his head angrily for a moment, staring out at the window, looking forlorn and pissed off as fuck. I let him be for now. Once we get back to the house, he'll watch the video, dominate my ass, probably add a few new scars, then he'll finally be out of his own head.

I hope.

8

~Gage~

*F*ucking Mason. *Fucking Mason and his fucking dick.* He knows who he belongs to. He knows not to fuck with that. Hell, I knew he was just getting back at me for not giving him what he begged for before he went on the trip.

But, this, this look of excitement, of hope, over a woman. *Ridiculous.*

I'm so pissed I can't even start to ask about the deal. My knee jitters up and down while I, instead, think about the thirty ways I'm going to tan his hide once we get home. After, of course, watching the video.

I need to see the woman that has him all tied up in knots like a fucking jackass.

"Sir, we're here." Our driver calls out, bringing me out of my anger-induced haze.

Shaking it off, I exit the Suburban and stomp my way up the concrete steps and through the double mahogany doors.

I can feel his presence behind me, so I don't bother shutting the door behind me. Instead, I stomp my way straight through the house, turn down the far hall, and make my way to the last door on the right. I flick the lights on and start unbuttoning my suit jacket almost robotically.

Hanging my jacket on the hook, I turn back toward the room just as Mason steps in behind me. I slowly start unbuttoning my shirt as I walk toward our sound system, flipping it on.

Pulling my phone from my pocket, I hit the YouTube Music app and hit my 'Danger' list. I need to clear my head, but first, I need the damn video.

The metal cover of Paparazzi by Leo blares through the speakers, dotting each corner of the room. I finish unbuttoning my shirt, slowly pull it from the confines of my pants, then shrug it off and toss it on the counter in front of me.

"Video." It's brash and cold, but he understands. He always understands. By the time I've unbuckled my belt, stripping it from the loops with one hand, my phone pings with an incoming message.

I wrap the belt around my right hand and pick up my phone. Turning on the TV and then clicking the screen mirror button on my phone, I click open the message and pull up the video. When I see his rogueish face staring into the camera, I pause the video and steady myself.

Closing my eyes to prepare for the visual assault, I take a deep inhale, then exhale and open them back up again. I quickly kick off my shoes while deftly unbuttoning and unzipping my pants, shucking them down to my ankles. I step out of my socks and pants at the same time and take a deep breath before turning around to face Mason.

My good little boy is already ass naked, standing in front of the St. Andrews cross, feet apart, head bowed, and hands behind his back.

Yup, he knows he's in trouble.

Fifteen minutes of silence later, my naughty boy is tied up to the cross. His head bows down, the red ball gag in his mouth already dripping with saliva as he tries and fails, repeatedly, to swallow his saliva. Thick, red leather cuffs secure his hands and feet, stretching him wide to match the x-shape of the cross.

Additionally, his nipples are clamped with small, alligator clip-like pinchers, bells dangling from each. His neck has two cords of hemp rope wrapped twice around it before trailing down his lean body over the planes of his rigid muscles. One wraps around his balls, not so tight to cut off complete circulation but tight enough to chafe if he moves too much. The other is wrapped around his dick in the same manner, keeping it nice and hard for me.

I walk back toward him with my favorite dagger and trail a fine, straight line down his peck, right through his nipple. He hisses in pain, and I watch in fascination as his muscles bunch from the pain. He starts trembling as he forces himself not to move too much; lest he yanks on his cock and balls.

With a smug smirk, I place the tip of the dagger under his chin and slowly nudge him to lift his head to meet my eyes. "Mine." I ground out through my teeth.

"Yor, Thir." He mumbles demurely around his ballgag.

"Damn, right you are." I spit with a growl. I retreat, marching over to my phone and clicking on play.

At first, I just see his face, smirking at the camera. Then, I hear a sweet little whimper right before he says, "Strip." His single command causes her to flinch a little. I have a decent view of her body, all plump and inviting. Her breasts are just over the perfect handfuls, and I see a few tattoos trailing down her leg and on her collarbone. I can't quite make out what they are due to the distance, but she is something else. That's for sure.

I can see her hands shaking as she peels off her top. "Stop!" He barks. "Slower. We have all night."

She tosses the bra over by his feet, and I hear the smug prick chuckle.

I see her stomach and arms flinch and bunch as she unbuttons, then unzips her pants and wiggles them down her sexy-as-hell curves' bringing her panties down with them.

Her panties don't even hit the floor before Mason is up and moving. A loud *smack*, immediately followed by a yelp, sounds out through the room. "You loopholed, Angel. You know better."

His gruff voice turns her on. I can tell. Her body flushes, her thighs squeeze together, and her cheeks pink up quite nicely.

I continue to watch their interaction, my dick hardening painfully in my briefs.

I chuckle lightly when he orders her to crawl on the bed, and she loses her footing before righting herself. Like a sexy little badass, she continues onto the bed, shucking her pants as she goes.

I get the perfect view of the right side of her body. Her ass is perfectly spankable, her tits perfectly squeezable, and her tattoos; good grief, I get why he's so tied up.

Something catches my eye on her left forearm. I barely catch it as she continues to crawl against the mattress.

Rewinding, I zoom in on the forearm, and my blood runs cold. Right there, in black outline, is a cross with the word 'grace' in script down the middle. I see 'Eph' but not the numbers. I can almost guarantee the numbers are 2:8. What really hits home is the blue and purple semicolon butterfly sitting in the top right corner.

It's her. Holy shit. It's fucking her!

I roar in frustration as I thud over to him. Grabbing hold of his jaw, I squeeze mercilessly.

I see his eyes hold actual, real fear in them, but the part of my brain that says to stop is turned off. Instead, the red haze of rage has settled over me.

"Tell. Me. Everything." I spit every fucking word, punctuating it with a squeeze of his jaw.

It takes me a minute to realize that he's snapping his fingers wildly, using his safeword because, *oh, duh,* he has a ballgag in...And I may actually be scaring him.

That thought, those sounds, cut through the red haze. I notice a trickle of blood dripping down his sneck from where the dagger pushed in a little. Everything rushes in, and I force myself to blink repeatedly. My brain quickly catches up, and I lean forward, ripping the clasps off the back of the ball gag and throwing it across the room. *Oh, shit. I got too lost. Too far gone. You're not supposed to play with high emotions. I mean, not this high.*

"I'm sorry," I utter, then repeat about ten more times as I quickly unwrap the ropes from his body and gently release him from the cuffs.

Once he's completely unhooked, untied, and unharmed, I lift him up and carry him to our large read leather sectional in the corner.

"I'm so sorry, Baby Boy," I murmur, folding his body against my chest as he sits in my lap. His stuttered breath causes my heart to break. *I did that.*

Real fear should never be in a scene. Period. This was a mistake.

I take my time, rubbing life back into his wrists, his ankles, and his neck. Inch by inch, his muscles relax into me until, finally, his breathing evens out.

Taking one of my hands, I gently guide his chin toward me, needing to look into those golden-hazel eyes. His grin is slight, rueful at best, but his eyes look clearer and devoid of the terror I saw there earlier.

"I'm sorry." I swallow audibly. "What do you need?"

His brows furrow slightly as he returns his knowing gaze to mine. "It's her, isn't it?"

The perceptive bastard knows I don't like talking about her. He knows better than to ask. But, judging by the look in his eyes, he deserves the answer.

With a heavy sigh, I drop my head to the back of the couch as I gently rub my other hand up and down his back, needing the comfort only he can bring.

After far too long, with just the sounds of Missio's Everybody Gets High playing through the room, I lean up, rub my hands roughly up and down my face, and look at the only man I've ever allowed myself to love.

My mouth opens and closes a few times. When nothing comes out, I force out a raspberry, and then... well, then I bare my soul to this beautiful man.

And it fucking hurts.

9

~Mason~

"So, what happens now?" I don't mean to sound like a child who just got grounded from his favorite toy, but, fuck...this sucks.

The question hangs in the air as Gage kills the music.

Walking over to me with that broad chest and those delicious tattoos momentarily distracts me from the heavy conversation we were having and the one we still need to have.

He's hiding something from me, but I don't know what. Yes, he told me that she had been a job and that her father is someone that Don is keeping an eye on. He told me how he fell for her and how she up and vanished one day. But, something, I don't know what, something niggles at the back of my mind. There's still something missing.

For now, I don't push it. I know he'll tell me when the time's right.

Gage plops down on the couch next to me and wraps his arm around my shoulders, allowing me to snuggle into him. His thumb traces idle patterns along my arm, and I take a moment just to breathe him in.

After what feels like forever in silence, he inhales audibly and pushes it back out. "Now, Mase, you'll have to do what I was instructed to do five years ago. You've gotta go back. You've gotta get as much intel on her as possible. Hell, maybe she knows more than what she lead on." He shrugs like that's all he can come up with, and I explode.

I sit up so fast that I almost fall right off the couch.

"Are you crazy? That's a terrible idea. She knew it was supposed to be one night that I was in town for business... How the hell am I going to get close enough to her to get all that? *She* was the one who didn't even want to give me her name." I rant while flailing my arms about.

"Mase...Mason, look at me." He soothes, rubbing a hand up and down my back to help center me.

I gulp and turn my head to find his striking blue eyes boring into me. He's no longer my Gage, or my Dom, he's my boss.

"Orders still stand. We need to find out everything we can about her. Keep an eye on her and anyone she's close to. Especially since her name is still on about a dozen hit lists."

He's right—I know he is—but to say I'm conflicted feels like an understatement. I really want to see her again, but not like this.

After a few moments of contemplation, I sigh, letting my head hang down between my shoulders and resting my elbows on my knees. "Alright. Fine. Let's do this."

Gage and I spent the rest of the afternoon hashing out a back story and sharing things he knew about her from before that could help me befriend her—like, she really loves egg rolls and despises spring rolls.

Then, we spent the evening having dinner and just being ourselves for a bit. I curled up into him on the couch with a large, fluffy blanket draped over us, watching Top Gun.

Of course, one thing turned into another and let's just say that today's plane ride is a little painful; but in the most phenomenal of ways.

A perky stewardess with long, red hair damn near slithers over to me. "Can I get you anything else, *sir*?"

Yuck. How desperate some people get when they think their target is rich is nauseating.

But I'm inherently not a dick to those who don't deserve it. So, I take the high road. "No, but thank you, though." I smile, then return back to scrolling through my phone.

I can physically feel her presence as she just stands there, hoping I'm joking or maybe in complete denial; I don't know.

Eventually, she huffs and turns around, heading back to the front of the plane.

The flight itself isn't terribly long, but it's just enough time to memorize my back story and come up with a few ideas on how to get close to her.

Worse comes to worse, I go to her club and watch her every night like a real damn stalker. But I'm hoping to save that level of creep as a backup to my backup.

The "fasten seatbelt" sign dings on, and the Captain's voice calls out through the speakers as we prepare to land.

My heart rate increases, and I feel a small smile stretch across my face at the thought of seeing my Angel again. The only problem is, will she be as excited to see me?

10

~Chloe~

The bar is rowdy for a Monday. We usually choose Sundays and Mondays to perform new skits, since it's relatively slower and gives the waitresses and bartenders time to help perfect our performance.

However, tonight has been loud; obnoxious even.

I step out on stage, the curtain still closed, and take my seat in the lone chair sitting front and center.

I worked my ass off yesterday, feeling better than I have in a long time after my, almost too intimate, encounter with Mason. The phantom feelings of his hands on my body, my pussy molding itself to his cock, and his deliciously sexy voice washes over me any time I stop moving for all of five seconds.

Damn, he was wonderful.

Suddenly, the MC calls my name, effectively bringing me out of my head. That Bitch by Bea begins playing out, and a wicked smirk takes over my face. The moment her first words are spoken, the curtains flare open, and the guys in the crowd whoop and holler out.

Leaning into the stigma of being Queen Bitch, I move my body to the music, singing out to the men in the crowd, grabbing hold of my breasts and squeezing my ass through my barely there booty shorts, while working my body to the music.

After a fancy little dip and spin, I whip my belt off and perform a crazy sequence I learned on TikTok. The crowd goes absolutely feral, and money starts flying over the stage.

By the end of the song, I'm sweaty and panting and on a high like no other. Being with Mason gave me back a little piece of confidence that I didn't know was missing. And, frankly, I'm here for it.

As the curtain falls, I quickly gather up the money that fell around me. There's so much that Alex and Carrie scurry out to help out so we can clear the stage for the next performance.

With a happy little sigh, I traipse back to my locker and quickly shove the money into my purse. I don't need to count it to know it's at least $200; that's if they were only throwing ones.

The rest of my shift went smoothly; no bumps or bruises, no major fights broke out, so overall, it was a fantastic Monday.

I'm just slipping into my street clothes when a knock comes from the locker room door.

"Hey, Grace..." Jo calls out through the bright ass pink door.

"Yeah, I'm coming! Give me two shakes." I giggle as I think about how I'm literally shaking my ass into these skin-tight, ripped black jeans.

Once I'm done, I quickly slide my feet into my black Converse slip-ons and throw a mesh black top over my black bra. The top is big and comfy and boasts a single skeletal hand holding a rose in the middle. I'm usually not a rose person, but this shirt was too hot for me to pass up. Between my high-waisted pants and my black sports bra, I look damn good. *Too bad it's being wasted on a drive-through clerk and a night in.*

Alas, such is my life.

Grabbing my purse and locking up my locker, I head to the Barbie pink door and swing it open to find Jo standing there looking all too serious for his usual happy-go-lucky personality.

"Something wrong?" I ask with a tilt of my head.

He flinches like I've caught him off guard. Like whatever was in his head had him sucked deep inside.

"Oh, um," He clears his throat and coughs a little, uncrossing his arms as he stands in front of me. "Just, this guy was looking at you weird. I don't know. I know I can be a little protective of all of you, but..." He trails off with a sigh, rubbing his hand down his face. "Just be careful, ok? I didn't like the way he was eyeing you. Ask me or one of the others to walk you out when you're ready. Deal?"

I scoff and roll my eyes. "Oh, Jo, you're so silly. It's probably just the guy from the other night. It's fine."

"Wait, what guy?" He grits out, probably pissed that I broke a club rule about not going home with guys from the club. *Fuck, I'm going to get fired.*

Holding my hands up, I try to placate him. "It was the guy who grabbed me at the end of my number two nights ago. I went to tell him off for giving me his number, but then I don't know..." I shrug and break eye contact, my face heating from embarrassment.

"Listen, I'm sorry. It won't happen again. I promise. I'm sorry." I heave a sigh and prepare to get reamed.

But, it never comes. Instead, he shakes his head, breathes in deeply with his eyes closed, then releases it. "Don't let it happen again." He snaps, pointing his finger right at my face. "Rules are there for a reason. Men are jealous, possessive bastards by nature. We don't need any of that shit in our club."

I'm already nodding like a bobblehead. "Yes, sir. I understand. It won't happen again."

Seeming to calm down a bit, he waves me away, wishes me a goodnight, and walks down the hallway toward the main area of the club.

I blow out a raspberry, feeling pretty damn shitty, then turn in the opposite direction toward the back entrance for the entertainers.

Stepping out into the cool evening, I take a moment to compose myself. I've never been reprimanded in any way, outside of the bedroom, since before my mother died. I was so scared to end up like her that I toed the goody-two-shoes line like a damn pro. Now, one sexy man with soulful eyes has sent me sprawling to the ground. *Fuck. This is why I don't date.*

Not that it was a date, per se, but same-same. Having a man in my life just isn't worth the hassle.

Just as the door clicks shut behind me, I look over to the security booth and see Bob on his phone, scrolling mindlessly on whatever app currently has his attention.

As I step off the curb, my phone buzzes in my pocket. Knowing better than to be caught off guard in the dark of night, I ignore it and jog over to my car.

As I get in and slam the door closed, I hit the lock buttons and then start pulling out of my space.

My phone vibrates in the drink holder with another incoming message, but I need just a little bit more time to read it.

Once I pull up to the security booth, I smile at Bob and tell him to have a good night. Overall, he's a nice-ish guy. But I feel like he's not actually paying attention to us or the patrons.

Like tonight, I barely get a grunt before he pushes the button for the security arm to lift out of the way.

I stop at the first red light and reach over, pluck my phone out of the cup holder, and click it on.

Ignoring the messages for now, I quickly click over to the YouTube Music app and find a random song to play on my ride home.

Just a Girl by No Doubt filters through the speakers and instantly brings a wide smile to my face. I spend my short car ride feeling free, confident, and amazing.

Until, of course, I park at my apartment and see that the messages...are from Mason.

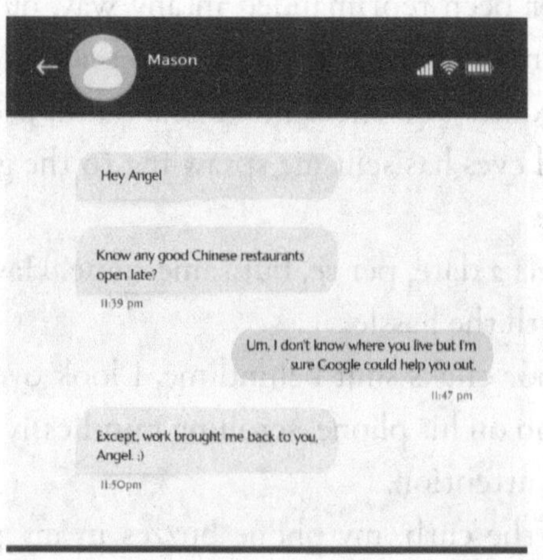

It takes far too long to suck in a shuttering breath as I blink away the shock of hearing from him again. And from the fact that he's back in town.

My pussy clenches involuntarily, and I suck my bottom lip into my mouth, biting hard enough to taste blood.

Instead of responding based on the beating of my clit, I grab my purse from under the seat and head inside my little one-bed, one-bath apartment.

Once the doors are firmly locked, I text back the name of my favorite late-night restaurant, then turn off the phone to decrease any temptation to actually entertain this man.

As I rush through my shower, I wonder why he's reaching out. I mean, we agreed to one night. One perfect, sexy night.

So, why not just find someone else to chat with? Why me?

11

~Mason~

I was happy to hear from Chloe last night, and the place she sent me to was amazing, but then I didn't hear from her again. I'm hoping it's because she was tired and *not* because she isn't interested in seeing me again. If that's the case, it's going to be very difficult to get close to her like I need to.

Clicking off the phone, I sit on the bed in the hotel and ponder the updated information we have about Chloe... I mean *Grace*.

She taught for barely a year while taking night shifts at *Big and Beautiful*. Then, she stopped teaching and now works 5, sometimes 6, times a week at the entertainment club.

I can't lie, it does something to me when I think about her, up on stage, dancing mostly naked in front of hundreds of people each week.

But, she loves it.

I could tell, just from that one number last week that it's about more than money. It's peace, acceptance, confidence...freedom.

Swallowing down a gulp of coffee, I exit the car and meander over to her apartment building; the one Gage just spent an hour grousing about.

Unfortunately, he's right. This place is a crap-shoot. I've been here for less than two minutes and have already slipped two cameras near the front of the building. With a gentle tug, the lock gives way and

I'm waltzing into the front lobby without so much as a security guard, front doorsman...nada.

I grind my teeth so hard that my jaw pops. I hate the lack of security but, thankfully, my Angel will be perfectly safe after I'm done. I just need to hurry up and place all of these cameras before she decides to leave the apartment for the day. I'm hoping that because she works late, she'll sleep late too.

I have covered every angle of her place, top to bottom, except for her actual apartment. That will have to wait until she leaves for her shift.

I'm back at the hotel and checking all of the cameras when my phone rings. Sliding the phone off the nightstand, I smile when I see that it's Chloe... *Angel. Keep it Angel, for now.*

I suck in a deep breath and stand from the bed just as I click on the green phone icon.

"Hello, Angel. Did you sleep well?"

Really? That's what you went with?

I shake off my obvious stupidity and soak up the sound of her giggle. Granted, she's giggling at me, but who cares?

"Um, I did. Thank you." She whispers out after she calms.

"But, that's not why I called..." She trails off. I can just imagine her biting on that plump lip of hers and have to hold back a groan as my dick hardens in my pants.

"Listen, um, I know you're here for business and all, but, um, do you maybe want to hang out? There's not a whole lot in town, but anything has to be better than the hotel. And, if you don't want to, that's fine and all-"

She's rambling a million miles a minute, and I let loose a chuckle before cutting off her clearly anxious ranting. "Ok, ok, Angel. Breathe for me. Just breathe."

I hear her immediately obey and have to thump my dick as it jumps with her obedience.

"Good girl," I coo. "Now, I would love to hang out with you. Whenever, wherever, I'm there."

I hear the sigh of relief on the other end of the line and smile to myself. My angel was nervous. She clearly doesn't put herself out there and has a lot of reservations. But she did it for me.

I feel a smile take over my face as we make plans to meet up on Saturday and spend the day together.

When we finally hang up, I text Gage with the update and immediately go to shower again. Yes, I showered this morning but, I want to be extra fresh after spending the morning surreptitiously placing cameras in and around her apartment building.

That, and, I really need to rub one out.

12

~Chloe~

I'm fiddling with the hem of my dress while sitting on the couch. Well, sitting makes it sound like I'm stationary. I'm far from that as I shift my legs underneath me, then let them fall to the ground before crossing them at the ankle...then lifting them up on the couch again.

Mason and I have texted every day this week and it's starting to feel more like a friendship than a hook-up. Or maybe more.

Shit, am I ready for more?

A series of knocks on the door brings me out of my anxiety just long enough for me to get tangled in my dress and stumble the entire way to the front door.

Finally righting myself, I wipe my sweaty hands down the front of my dress and fluff my hair out before unlocking the door.

Swinging it open, I almost choke on my own spit. Mason is standing there in a light blue button-up shirt with the top buttons undone, showing off that sexy chest of his. He's in a pair of drool-worthy jeans and black Chucks, which immediately makes me smile.

"Angel, you look..." His eyes sweep up and down my body appraisingly, and I feel myself blushing from the attention. This man has seen me naked, but this feels so much more vulnerable.

Clearing my throat, I duck my head and try to hide the smile creeping over my face.

"So, shall we?" I mumble while moving forward.

"Oh, yes. Um, after you." He swings his arm out like he's trying to be a gentleman and I giggle out when I notice that he winces and shakes his head.

Stepping forward, I close the door, lock it up, and head toward the stairs, eager to start the date.

No, not date. Um, outing. Hang out?

By the time my internal freakout is finished, we're walking out of the lobby and into the chilly air.

Stopping on the sidewalk, I turn to face Mason and catch him ogling my ass. He tries really hard to cover it up but fails miserably, and we both end up chuckling.

"So, we have options. There is a fair in town, but there's also a movie. What's your poison?" I try for nonchalant, but I'm pretty sure the rambling overshadowed that.

"Do you have work tonight?" He asks with a tilt of his head.

Shaking my head, I bite my lip and exhale. "Noooo." I elongate the word, wondering where he's going with this.

"Then, why choose?"

He quirks his brow as he says his words, and I swear he says, "Why choose?" with more than a little meaning behind it, but that may just be because that's the kind of book I read.

Shaking the thoughts of being between him and another man, I swallow heavily and loop my arm into his. "You're right. Fair first, then movie?"

"Sounds good to me, Angel. But first, I need your name."

My eyes go round, and I realize that he's never asked. Well, I didn't give him much of a choice, either.

"Grace. My name's Grace." The lie rolled right off my tongue, and, for the first time in years, it tasted sour in my mouth.

For some reason, I have an overwhelming need to tell him the truth. My truth.

With a smile, he walks me down the sidewalk, completely impervious to my inner turmoil. His smile is so wide, so inviting that I push my feelings down and remind myself that he's here for business, for just a short amount of time...and there's no way in hell I'm risking my past catching up with me just because this man causes my brain to short-circuit.

Instead, I talk to him about when Jo and some other co-workers attended the fair last year. He cracked up when I told him Alex ate too much funnel cake before getting on the tilt-o-whirl, causing her to throw up on herself and the poor man sitting next to her.

For the rest of the night, we laughed, ate, and talked. He seems to be more than happy to share about himself, except regarding his job. But, hey, it's the first time we're hanging out so it's no big deal.

The smile on my face doesn't disappear for the rest of the night, and something warm keeps lighting in my belly, but I'm choosing to ignore that little feeling for now.

<h1 style="text-align:center">13</h1>

<h1 style="text-align:center">~Chloe~</h1>

It's been four weeks since Mason and my first official date. Although, neither of us said it was such. However, I did end the night with a belly full of funnel cakes, a stuffed sloth that is almost as large as I am, and a toe-curling orgasm in the back of the theatre while some random thriller played on the screen.

Since then, I've seen Mason every night. Sometimes, it's only for a short time, as his business keeps him really busy. But he always takes time to meet me at my job and walk me to my car or drive me home. And, I usually end up in bed, or on the couch, or bent over a chair.

The man has re-activated my healthy libido, that's for sure.

And, as luck would have it, I'm making more money than I've ever imagined. Apparently, a healthy sex life is good for my dancing. I'm making almost double the amount I usually do, and it's doing wonders for my self-esteem and confidence.

My number just finished, and I'm smiling so wide that my face hurts.

Jo walks around the curtain and lifts me while spinning around. "Damn, girl! That was hot as fuck! You almost convinced me to leave Mikey and try pink tacos." I laugh at his exuberance and slap his back until he sets me down.

"Whoever he is, better keep 'em around." He whispers while hugging me tight.

Once he backs away, I see the gleam in his eyes and shake my head. "Who says it's a guy?"

He laughs me off, turns me toward the dressing room, and swats my ass. "Get some rest, pretty girl. I expect you to keep bringing in the big bucks this weekend." He calls out from behind me.

The girls cheer as I walk into the locker room. I playfully curtsy, then roll my eyes as they holler and wolf-whistle.

"Damn girl, that was fucking hot! Maybe you should just be in charge of all of our numbers." I blush at Claire's statement and brush them off.

Pushing through them, I open my locker and take out my phone, silently hoping that Mason is already here.

But, unfortunately, there's nothing.

I try to push away the sting of disappointment, but it proves to be a clingy bastard.

It's not like we're even dating, or going out, or whatever.

Rolling my eyes at myself, I stuff the cash from my last number into my bag and quickly change.

I really want to get out of here and take a shower. My new number has me working up quite a sweat. That, and the club has been freaking packed all week! Like, wall-to-wall packed. But I refuse to complain because the tips have been phenomenal.

Closing my locker, I say bye to the girls and text Mason, letting him know that I'm on my way home and I'll call him later.

I hit the exit bar for the staff door, and the brisk chill of the incoming Fall storm feels refreshing on my overheated skin.

As I walk toward my car, a familiar prickle of unease sweeps through me. The hairs on the back of my arms and neck stand to attention, and I quickly do a visual sweep of the lot around me. Only employees are supposed to park back here. But that doesn't mean the occasional drunken asshole doesn't end up stumbling over to this side.

I look over at the security gate and see that Bob is currently reading something on his phone. *Always on his damn phone.*

I consider, for two seconds, calling out for Bob to walk with me, but a car backfiring on the road causes me to yelp and run straight through the lot. I probably look like an idiot running for my life with no one chasing me, but who gives a damn.

When I get to my car, I unlock it, hop in, and slam the door, immediately hitting the lock button. I don't bother with my phone or music; I just jam the key into the ignition and move to shift into gear.

A thick, coarse rope being wound around my neck has me suddenly panicking and gasping for breath.

Fear and adrenaline race through my body as I struggle against my attacker's hold. *Fucking* backseat. *I should have checked! Dammit.*

My attacker leans forward; the smell of stale cigarettes and gin assaults my senses as he licks, actually fucking licks, a path from the base of my neck to my ear.

"Nice to meet you, Princess." He grits out, his Russian accent thick as I continue to shift and flail in his hold.

I struggle for a moment..., and then an old movie scene comes to me. I don't bother questioning it. My vision is blurry and dotting on the sides, and my mind is almost too foggy to think.

I take one hand off the rope around my neck, just long enough to put my foot on the brake and pop the car into drive. Then, I ram my foot down on the accelerator.

The car lurches forward and I'm briefly thankful that I reversed into my parking spot today.

Of course, those happy thoughts end pretty quickly as we fly through the lot and crash head-on with the cement wall that separates our lot from the business next to us.

The movement forces the man behind me to careen forward between the seats, causing the rope to go slack around me.

I suck in greedy lungfuls of air as I unlock the door and fall out into the lot. I try to scream, but nothing comes out; my throat is far too bruised from him yanking so hard.

The man in my car roars in agony and frustration, reminding me that I need to fight through the fog and adrenaline and get up.

I'm face-down, staring at the concrete, vision doubling... but I do it. I push myself to stand and start to shakily run toward the security gate. How he didn't hear the commotion is beyond me, but I swear Bob is so getting fired.

I'm rounding the back of my car when I vaguely hear my attacker grunting and plopping out of the car. I briefly look back, wobbling on my feet and praying I can get them to move faster.

By the time I turn around, I'm smacking headfirst into a lean, hard body. I scream out and barely register another man running past us, roaring with such intensity that I wince. The man in front of me now has me wrapped up in his arms and, although I struggle, and scream, and fight, he doesn't loosen up. Instead he...*shushes me?*

That can't be right.

I vaguely process the sounds of grunts and groans behind me and realize that the man holding me may just be Bob. He's here to help.

I gradually stop fighting, my body trembling from fear and exhaustion as the man holding me continues to rub his hands up and down my arms and murmurs, "It's ok. I've got you, Angel. You're ok."

Wait, what? Angel?

I'm terrified, hurt, tired, and fucking hungry but, right now, all of that goes away. I gradually lift my head off the man's chest to get the first glimpse of my savior.

"Mason?" I squeak incredulously. Also confirming that my voice-box is, in fact, damaged.

He grins as he looks down on me, brushing away blood or tears or something wet off of my cheeks with his thumb.

"I'm here, Angel. And, I uh..." He coughs out, looks at someone behind me, and nods once. "I brought a friend."

Gently, he begins to turn me toward the men behind me.

One is standing tall, proud, bloody, *pissed.*

The other, who I know to be my attacker, is lying in a pool of his own blood. Completely out cold. *Or dead.*

I flick my eyes up to the man standing. The shadows of the lot make it impossible to see his face.

That is, until he takes one step forward into the light.

"Gage?!" I choke out.

Then, my world is shrouded in darkness.

14

~Mason~

"Fuck, fuck, fuck." I pace the private plane, the same one I was on a month ago, and pull at my hair. "Shit. Fuck. I mean. Fuck, man. What did we just do?"

Gage sips from his glass tumbler filled with whiskey, calm and eerily cool given the circumstances. His expression is blank, but I can see the whirlpool of emotions swirling through his eyes. His suit jacket is unbuttoned, showing off his light blue shirt. His perfectly pressed, black slacks don't even have a tiny bit of lint on them, even after the scuffle and disposal of the joker who actually thought he could kidnap Grace.

I mean Chloe.

Or...should I say, the Traitor's Princess?!

Yeah, Gage decided to drop that bomb when he randomly showed up at the hotel this evening, freaking out. Apparently, the Russians have finally caught up to Chloe and planned to take her tonight. And that was when he chose to tell me that she's not just someone who Don thinks has valuable information. No. She's the Traitor's daughter! The infamous traitor that's been making moves against the Don for years before I came along.

Once Gage got me through the initial shock, we planned to confront Chloe, tell her she was in danger, and, hopefully, talk her into coming back home with us.

Instead, we walked into her being attacked; then she fainted in my arms. Once Gage walked over to us, he pulled out a syringe and stuck it in her neck before stating, "Well, that didn't go as planned. Let's get her on the plane."

I won't lie: it took me a moment, or three, to process his command before he clapped his hand on my shoulder. "Gotta go, Mase. The guard won't be out much longer, and clean up is two minutes out."

My brain caught up just enough to lift her in my arms, bridal style, and follow Gage around the corner, sliding into the still-running car.

Now that we're on the plane, the information overload from today is overwhelming my brain.

Chloe's the Traitor's Princess.

We're kidnapping the Traitor's Princess.

I fucked the Traitor's Princess!

Oh Fuck.

"Fuck. What did *I* do?!" I feel the familiar tightness of my chest and the faint black circles dancing in my vision. I'm going to have a panic attack.

Suddenly, a sharp, commanding bark breaks through my panic. "Breathe. Sit down. Have a drink." Gage states unflappably. There is no room for argument, and at this moment, I'm thankful for his domineering side.

I slam into the seat across from him and rest my elbows on my knees, slide my fingers through my hair, and groan in frustration.

The sound of glass sliding across a plastic table has me popping my head up, just a little, to peer at him in time to see him settling back into his seat, a darkly serious look on his face.

"We did what we had to do." He says dispassionately.

"And why didn't you ever mention who she actually is? All this time? You had been shacking up with the Boss' enemy?!" I spit, abruptly standing to start pacing again. "And, to make matters worse, you sent me to…"

"I didn't tell you to fall for her!" He screams out.

Then, with a blink of an eye, he runs his hand down his chest and continues.

"Besides, Don knew. I was sent to… monitor her once we found her identity." His tone is annoyingly casual like we're discussing the weather. "Things progressed, and well, the Boss didn't mind. Especially since she had made it abundantly clear that she had zero ties with her father. All she knows is that he took off when her mother got pregnant, and her mother had never told her who it was." Gage shrugs a shoulder like it's no big deal and takes a large gulp of his whiskey.

I can feel the rage building in my system, deep in my bones, and I know it's about to boil over. "You didn't fuckin' tell me! All this time… years, Gage, years! And you never told me!"

"She was off limits!" He explodes out of his chair. "She fucking left! Just up and disappeared. Then, then, you came along and, well, *that,* and what do you want from me?! To point out that not only did the only woman I ever loved completely skip out on me, but that I was in charge of keeping an eye on her? What the fuck do you want from me?!" He yells out again, deciding to pace as well, and pulls the long hair at the top of his head roughly.

The stewardess decides to walk in, letting us know that the plane is about to begin its descent. With a firm nod, Gage swallows audibly, rubs his hands down his shirt- as if there were any wrinkles- and takes his seat. He swallows the rest of the amber liquid in his glass then sets it down, exhales heavily through his nose, and stares out the window.

Great, I guess that's the end of that conversation.

I take my spot across from him, also staring out the window, and wonder where the hell we're going to go from here.

It's been two hours since we landed. I'm nursing a beer and so angry that I can't even see straight. If things weren't bad enough, the overbearing asshole locked her in a room and installed a series of stupid-as-fuck deadbolts to make sure she can't escape.

I scoff through my teeth.

Escape.

Shaking my head, I sigh and let my head hang between my shoulders, staring at the wood floors below me.

Of all the women, it had to be her. It had to be fucking *her.*

I hear Gage's bare feet walking down the stairs; *thip-thapping* as he goes. My ears twitch as he continues toward the living room, headed straight for the chair next to where I'm sitting.

The leather screeches underneath his weight, and I swear my head burns from the force of his stare. But I'm in no mood for his psycho-babble bullshit tonight.

I hear him shift forward, probably mirroring my position with his elbows resting on his thighs.

"Don't," I grunt out, picking at the corner of the beer bottle.

"Mase…" He murmurs.

I stand so fast that some of my beer sloshes over the side. "No, Gage," I spit like his name is a curse: like he's a curse.

Stomping in the opposite direction, I head toward the kitchen, gulping the last half of my beer as I go.

"Mase. Just listen." He commands like the arrogant son-of-a-bitch he is.

I grit my teeth, sure that my teeth are going to turn into dust within the next five minutes. And I can feel a tension headache building just between my shoulder blades and the base of my skull.

Waving the bottle past the sensor, I toss the bottle into the trash and let it automatically close as I pass through the kitchen to the fridge.

Ripping the door open, I zero in on the beer on the second shelf and grab one. Uncapping it, I take a deep pull before slamming the fridge shut with my foot.

Of course, that means Gage is now face-to-face with me. "Mason. You're being ridiculous. She needs to be here. She's safest here. Take your dick out of the picture, and you know I'm right." He snarls at the end, likely more upset that I've fucked his mystery girl than anything else.

"What- the fuck-ever, man. Leave my dick out of it. I can't help that she wanted *me* and ran from *you*."

I rise to my full height, which is still a couple of inches shorter than he is. I can feel my nostrils flare, and I'm sure if I were a cartoon, there would be smoke billowing from both of my ears.

"Fuck you, Mase! One night. You had one fuckin' night with her and came back here with that stupid fucking look in your eyes like you had magically met the one."

"Oh, screw you! You've been pining over her for years-" I thrash my arm to the side, off in the general direction of the room she's currently held prisoner in.

"Exactly!" He screams in my face. "She's mine! Always has been, always fucking will be."

The words hit harder than they should. A fiery ball of shame and hurt burns within my heart. When Gage came along, I was grappling with the loss of my first boyfriend. Like, first ever boyfriend. I had plenty of girlfriends before him, but putting myself out there, really submitting to my bisexual desires, the desire to just be with whomever I care about without prejudice, was terrifyingly hard.

But Gage. Gage with all his masculine glory, his boss-man attitude, Gage with his muscles and seriousness...Gage claimed me, body, mind, and soul faster than I could even try to figure out how to flirt with such an intimidatingly sexy man.

Now, he's standing here in front of me, ripping through my heart by confirming what I've always, quietly known: I'm nothing more than a placeholder for *her*.

Sharing women was one thing, being together, another. But, now that she's here, that's all gone.

It's all gone, and I'm stuck out in the cold, naked and alone.

Blinking back the tears that want to fall, I nod my head solemnly a few times, breathing in deeply. My jaw tightens as his eyes flick between mine. "Ok. You're right. *Boss.*" I sneer, shoulder-checking him as I pass and head toward my room.

How the hell did one girl simultaneously bring me the most joy- and the most pain- I've ever known?

15

~Gage~

Chloe fucking Rossi. The only woman to ever have my heart. And the only one to completely shred it apart.

I blow a raspberry through my lips as I fall onto my bed, dropping an arm across my eyes.

Chloe fucking Rossi.

The hurt she caused me was far more than the hit to my pride when she skipped town for no apparent reason. It was more than the bullshit hoops I've had to jump through because I failed as a capo and am now a button. And it was more than the fear I'd felt for years, wondering if her asshole father was holding her. Her leaving, completely disappearing, left me with a gaping hole that no amount of booze or torture could fill.

Her father, a leader of one of the most powerful families North of here, formed a coup and went into hiding and has been making moves against my Don ever since.

Apparently, he put his pregnant wife in Witness Protection and ran off in an entirely different direction.

Dom says it's taken years to track them down. Once they were sure it was the missing Italian queen and princess, *I* was sent.

As a capo, climbing the ranks rather quickly and in my early twenties, I scoffed at the notion of being a glorified babysitter.

"Just keep an "eye" on her, and determine if she knows anything about her piece of shit father." Those were Don's words, and you never say "no" to Don.

Then, well, then shit got complicated. It was apparent very quickly that she had no idea who her father was. But, more than that, she was *everything.*

Soft and naive, yet hard and unyielding.

There was always a fire in her eyes, like the things her mother put her through hardened her just a little. That damn woman walked through life with a smile as bright as the sun, would give you the last dollar to her name, but she didn't take any shit from anyone.

Including me.

She's always had curves for days, but now...

I bite on my knuckles, groaning as I roll to my side. Now she not only has curves, but she fucking owns them. And I'll be damned if it's not the most attractive thing about this new Chloe.

It appears the days of her hiding behind baggy sweaters and jeans are long gone. Seeing her tonight- last night now, I guess- made it perfectly clear that the hot little number she wore for Mason in that video wasn't a one-time thing. Watching her stumble out of the car in barely there top and skin-tight jeans, yeah...it took a minute to remember she had been in danger and that fucker needed to pay.

And he did, and then she fucking fainted.

Ugh! How she whispered my name like I was the last person she expected; like I was the last person she ever wanted to see, gutted me.

Fuck.

My phone incessantly buzzes on the nightstand. I want to ignore it. I want to get rip-roaring drunk and drown the memories of Chloe that are always floating just below the surface.

Alas, I don't have that luxury. Not when you're working for one of the most feared mafia bosses in the US.

I lean up, grumbling under my breath, and swipe my phone from the nightstand. I'm suddenly glad I didn't ignore it like I wanted to, as the messages are all coming from the Don.

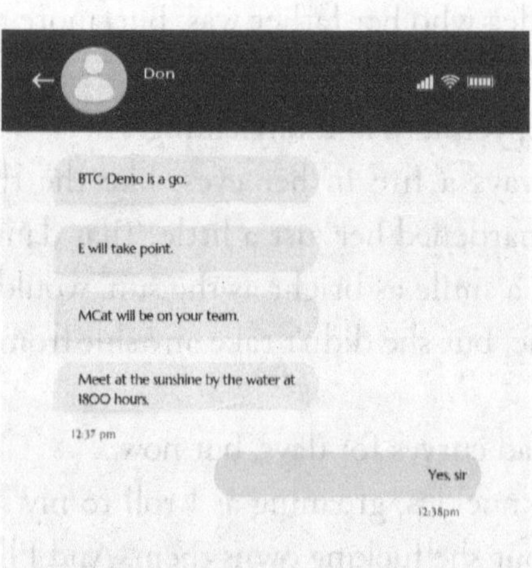

With a heavy sigh, I scrub a rough palm up and down my face, allowing the push and pull of my skin to ground me.

With another deep inhale, I pull up Mason's number and stare at it for far too long.

Mason has been my everything for two years. He brought out a side of my sexuality I never knew existed. Hell, my feelings for him far outweigh any feelings I've had for others.

Except her.

But, still...they aren't the same. These, these, feelings.

My feelings for both of them are vibrant and bold, intoxicating and overwhelming, but in completely different ways.

Mason consumes my mind; his dark and twisted ways mirror mine. He accepts me wholly for the monster I am, and sex with him is like a star imploding.

But Chloe consumes my heart to the point where sanity and insanity dance together in a macabre, impending train wreck. Sex with her is like a star being born. It's explosive and all-encompassing, burning bright for all to see.

Hell, I even dominate them differently. I go a lot harder on Chloe than I ever have, Mason. While they both love to be tied up in intricate designs, Mason's bindings are always tight and force him to be completely immobile. There's something about watching his muscles bunch and bulge with each touch that sends tingles down my spine.

Chloe, on the other hand, looks beautiful with her curves trussed up on display. But, allowing movement within the bindings, having the whole system moving, is like watching art in motion. The way her body writhes and ripples into and away from various touches is purely intoxicating.

I roughly shake my head to clear out the memories as I palm my chest, hoping to ease the current ache.

Clicking over to Mason's number, I send the message. He can be pissed all he wants but we've been called in to help another family with a gang takeover.

And these assholes are running women.

Biting the inside of my cheek to keep my emotions in check, I type out a quick message.

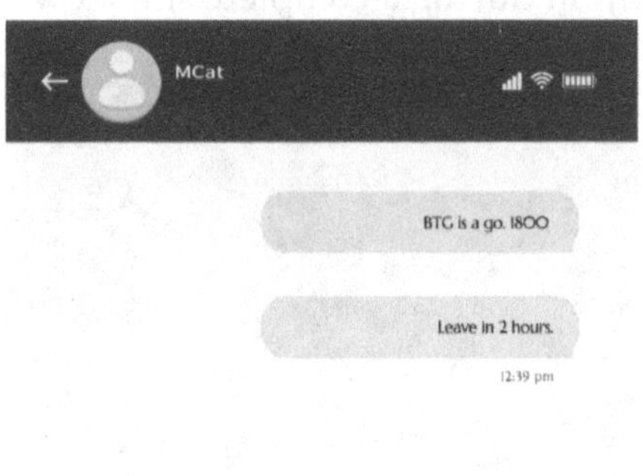

I stare at the phone until I see that he has, in fact, read the message.

Wow. He really is pissed.

Fuck, this is not the time for all this drama. Only Chloe could cause so much turmoil during a complete shitshow.

16

~Chloe~

Consciousness knocks against my eyelids, but I can't gather enough oomph to let it through.

My stomach rolls with indecision, and my head pounds like a bass drum.

Slowly, oh so slowly, I blink my eyes open and immediately squeeze them shut. The light coming from... somewhere... is obnoxious this early in the morning. Well, probably afternoon since my work hours are weird.

I heave a sigh and try to remember if I went out last night. I mean, my shift ended a couple of hours before closing time, but this sure the hell feels like worse than any hangover I've ever had.

But, last night...it's so foggy.

Suddenly, my eyes spring open, and my mind flips through the groggy images of last night.

The man in the car trying to kill me.

Crashing my car.

Mason.

And...and.

Oh fuck!

Gage found me!

I have to run again. I can't stay here! I have to move- now!

I push past the nausea and whip the blanket off my body. The room's chill causes my flesh to ripple with goosebumps, and I vaguely process that I'm in the same outfit from last night.

It takes me a minute of deep concentration to get my legs to move, and my knees and quads quake from the effort. Eventually, though, I stand and fumble my way toward the door to my left.

I trip over my feet just as I reach the brass handle and stumble into the door, crashing my shoulder into the unforgiving wood. Crying out in pain, I slide down to the floor, grasping onto my shoulder and willing my aching head and nausea to go away.

Breathing deeply- in, out, in, out- my blurry vision begins to re-align, signaling that it's time to get up. Time to try again.

My body shivers as the war of pain pumps to and from all directions, but I push through it until I'm standing once more. Knob in hand, I give it a good tug. But nothing other than the jolt of my elbow joints pinching happens. So, I try again. The knob doesn't turn. It doesn't click. It barely wiggles within its little hole in the respite gray wooden door.

I tilt my head as I consider the door. The one that's locked from the outside. The one that is a different color from the solid white doors in my apartment.

Dread roils through my stomach as I close my leaking eyes, tears steadily running down my face. I mechanically turn around to face the room. The one that isn't mine.

No, this isn't mine at all.

I swallow the lump in my throat, feeling the pocket of nerves squeeze down my esophagus as I take in the room surrounding me.

I shakily take in the cool blue bedding covered with a steel gray comforter that I haphazardly threw off of me.

The alabaster-painted walls are subtle, simple, much like the rest of the room. There's a single window, latched and barred. I'm not even sure why there's a window because, other than sunlight, you can't see anything through it. It reminds me of the glass panes they purposefully blur in bathrooms so people can't see in.

Unfortunately, that's it.

There's not a nightstand, a dresser, a shelf, or even a chair. Just a lone, queen-sized bed facing the door and a useless window on the right wall.

It's at this moment that I realize two things: I've been taken. I've been taken by my murderous ex-boyfriend.

So, I do what most stupid women would do. I scream.

I yell, I thrash, I punch holes in the walls.

I fucking scream!

If he thinks he can just kidnap me and get away with it, he's got another thing coming.

17

~Mason~

We're about to leave for this side mission, but I've been busy in the kitchen trying to put together a little snack and drink tray for Chloe.

Yeah, *Chloe*. Now I can call her by her real name. None of this fake nonsense.

I realize that I'm grinning and immediately force my whole face to relax. Business first.

Pfft. Right business. There is nothing business about this whole ordeal. Fuck me.

After finishing an overly large sandwich on a buttery croissant and dumping three handfuls of different chips, I grab a bottle of water and a Coke, just in case.

We're going to be gone for a few hours at least, and I don't want her starving. That would just be inhospitable.

Again, I chuff sarcastically at my own mind. I'm pretty sure the last thing she's going to worry about is whether or not we're hospitable. But, the time we spent together this last month meant something; means something. And I'll be damned if she ever thinks differently.

Just as I'm eyeballing a bowl of strawberries, I hear a bloodcurdling scream. My heart plummets to my ass as I hightail it through the kitchen, barely stepping through the foyer and running down the hall-way.

The sound of wall-rattling thuds, angry murmurs, and screeching screams assault my ears as I work on the four stupid-ass deadbolts that Gage put on this door.

Just as I open the door, a fist flies into my face, catching me off guard and landing straight in my jaw. By the time the next blow comes, I'm ready for it. I block it with my forearm, then latch onto her wrist, yank her arm behind her back, twirl her around, pinning her up against the wall.

"Calm down, Angel," I grunt low in her ear as she thrashes her head and her legs.

"Chloe. Stop!" I bark, pushing her a little harder against the wall.

"Fuck off!" She spits the curse at me and continues to fight to free herself from my grip.

"Chloe, Angel. There's a lot you need to know. But you're safe here."

Her body immediately goes lax at my words and I can practically hear the cogs in her head turning. "Listen, we have to leave. We have, um, some people who need help, and we won't be back until morning. But I have some food for you and I was going to ask if you wanted a book or something to keep you busy until we can have a proper ta-alk."

My last word is cut by her head, nailing me in the side of the face.

Damn! Naughty girl fights dirty. Fuck.

This is not the time for a boner.

Shaking it off, I wrench her arm while I step back and twirl her around with me so I can scoop her up and toss her on the bed. She hits the bed with a bounce, her eyes wide in disbelief and a little bit of intrigue, but I don't have time for this.

I'm already halfway out the door when I call back, "I'll bring you a few books and the food up in five minutes. Please don't make this harder than it has to be, Angel."

And with that, I close the door, quickly lock the deadbolts, and stride back to the kitchen.

My knee bounces with pent-up energy as we near our destination.

Some friends of ours with the Cosa Nostra needed some *help* with eradicating a local gang. Not to brag, but as one of the most infamous enforcers of the Italian mafia, they reached out to our Don and asked if we Gage and I could lend a hand.

At first, Don is hard-pressed to send two of his best guys frolicking through a gang war, until he finds out it isn't a gang war at all.

Some douche canoes who call themselves the Black Thorns Gang decided to procure Cosa Nostra shipments and use their barge to traffick women.

Not something we are ok with.

Guns; sure.

Drugs; fine. Your body, your choice, and all that.

But women and children; that's a hard, *indisputable*, hell no.

Apparently, Enzo got involved because a group of guys came looking for help to find their kidnapped girlfreind. And all signs pointed to the douche canoe who runs the gang.

We pull into the lot of a random hotel and silently check our weapons, concealing them all in our waistbands, under our pant legs, and I even have a few knives strapped to my forearms under my long-sleeve shirt.

We finish, completely in sync, and pause to look at each other. We usually banter, possibly take bets about who is going to take out the most people, and generally joke with each other.

But, with everything going on with Chloe, and the fact we're saving trafficking victims... neither of us is in a joking mood. Instead, I swallow loudly and nod my head at him. He does the same, turns to open the door, then quickly steps out of the truck, closing the door without a backward glance.

Shaking my head, I exhale heavily through my nose, then follow his lead, stepping out of the truck and slamming the door a little harder than necessary.

Following a step behind him, we make our way through the large sliding glass doors and straight to the elevators.

Crowding in with a few others, I notice a couple of them look all too familiar with blending in. Nudging Gage subtly, I dart my eyes to my left to indicate my concern.

His brows furrow, just barely, before he clears his throat and fiddles with his skin-tight black Henley, perfectly molded to each of his muscles.

The men behind us shift, just enough to notice but not so much as to draw attention.

In the blink of an eye, Gage slams the button on the electronic board, causing the elevator to screech to a halt. We simultaneously turn, flicking guns out of our waistbands, and pin the two men standing behind us with our forearms bulging against their throats.

Gage's gun is trained on the man he has pinned, while mine is trained on the bastard next to me.

I'm standing nose-to-nose with a man who absolutely fits the bill of trying too hard to fit in. He looks like he should be in the UFC and not in some half-rate hotel near Kemah.

With a smirk, I tilt my head, allowing him to see my crazy. But this motherfucker, here, just rolls his eyes.

Gage, who's his usually deathly silent self tilts his head and blinks once. "Why are you here?" His voice is low, calm, and gives even me chills from the amount of malevolence dripping from each word.

"Enzo." Is all the other man can choke out. Although, he isn't struggling. He's taking Gage's brute strength and is barely blinking.

Damn, these guys are fucking good.

Glad they're on our side.

With a barely perceptible nod, Gage and I immediately drop our arms, release the men from our holds, and holster our guns. Gage sticks his hand out in a sign of peace and, after a brief shake, turns and pushes the red button.

And, like the badass that he is, he just stands there, hands shoved into his pockets like he didn't have a care in the world.

Crazy bastard.

Unfortunately, he's strung so tight that I'm sure these men won't be the first ones to see Gage's silent crazy. The thought causes me to smirk because- what can I say- I love to see Gage's crazy side.

18

~Gage~

The room is far too packed for my liking but, seeing as we're all here for the same reason, I'm trying to adjust to it.

Enzo is a force in his own right- we've all heard the stories- but realizing he's here to help someone he doesn't even know makes me respect him more. I'd be interested to see how he runs things up North.

Just after Enzo introduces everyone, we get to work. Mason and I will be working together with Team Beta; the group going to the warehouse where they keep the girls and other trafficking merchandise.

A knock on the door puts all of us on edge as we wait for one of the other guys to check the peephole. His hand swipes downward in a signal to stand down.

With bated breath, we all watch as he opens the door and allows four ridiculously fit men inside.

One man is bigger than I am. He's about my height with brown, unkempt hair, a fantastic beard, and a build that screams SWAT.

The man who walks in right behind him is already passing him to set up at the table across the room. His blue hair is dull and faded, shaved close to the sides and longer on top. His facial hair is more of a couple of days stubble that he just hasn't bothered to do anything with.

The other two men are similar in build and height, just a couple of inches shorter than me with long, lean muscles that twitch as they take in the rest of us. One guy has long, gorgeous hair, and the other has his shaved close and longer on top.

I'm not sure who these men are, but it's glaringly obvious that they aren't usually on this side of the law.

I wonder if they're the ones who know the missing girl?

Enzo quickly makes introductions, and we find out that they are, in fact, with the girl who's being trafficked by these assholes. And they look downright murderous.

An hour later, we're all staggering down the stairs on either side of the building. Unfortunately, the blue-haired guy found out that the girls had been moved already, sending the four of them into a mini-tail spin. Thankfully, they appear to all be back on board and remember that the Cosa Nostra will be on the receiving end of these bastard's shipment.

Lucky for us.

Unlucky for them.

Mase and I hop into the "electric company" van while the others split off into their assigned roles and modes of transportation.

Comms begin sounding off as we do one last weapons check.

Even though Mase and I are on the outs at the moment, I know he's got my back, and he knows I have his. Period.

Once we get the all-clear, we take off.

Mase and I are following Enzo's group to a warehouse building where the gang reportedly holds their merchandise; including the women they *just* transported back. Enzo got word that something must have happened because the shipment was delayed and they returned back to the warehouse.

Perfect.

My knuckles are white against the steering wheel the closer we get.

Thoughts of Chloe being taken fill my mind, and I would bet money that Mason's thinking about it, too.

It didn't take long to find out that these men are simple gym owners: one is a police officer for fuck's sake! Whoever this girl is, she must really be special. It's obvious they love her, but not everyone would hop the line of morality for someone they love.

I gotta hand it to them, it's ballsy as fuck, and I like it.

It feels like I've barely blinked, and we're already here. We turn off the van and wait for instructions as we're on standby.

Moments later, a bone-jarring *boom* rattles the windows, and Mason laughs. Crazy fuck always did love a good show.

I gaze over at him, a small smile playing on my face as he meets my gaze. A million tiny conversations pass between us before he finally nods, reaches over the console, and squeezes my hand.

Suddenly, I feel the weight of relief lift off my shoulders and instantly take in a deep breath.

The familiar ta-ta-ta of gunshots can be heard from the lot, and we get the command to move.

Turning the engine over, I flip us around and park sideways in front of the door-er, um- hole in the wall. Mason quickly jumps out and slides the back van door open, allowing easy access for the others.

Just then, a shot rings out, and Mason drops to the ground outside the van.

I roar out, pushing my door open and chasing the mother fucker who dared to shoot at him.

Four bullets later, you know, just in case, and that fucker is down.

Lingerie-clad women are being escorted to the other van, and I rush to Mason. "Mase! Mase! Come on, Baby. Open your eyes." I encourage, slapping his face a little.

He rouses, sort of- his eyes fluttering open and closed- then his head lolls backward again.

Knowing we're in the medic van, I take his upper body into mine and lift him up and over the lip of the van. Once his back is stable, I hop in and drag him further into the opposite side.

Our supplies are in giant duffle bags, so I rip one open and fling out packs and packs of gauze.

"Hang in there, Mase. Come on."

Just as I finish packing his wound, another man is being hoisted into the van by one of Enzo's men. I recognize him as one of the four searching for their girl. *Dammit.*

Hopping up, I help get him situated in the van and hear a last call through the comms.

I continue packing the other guy, Cory, and hurriedly jump out of the van, rushing to the other side. Mason and Cory need doctors, and soon.

Just as I'm about to jump in, the long-haired guy hops into the van, scoops his friend into his arms, and starts whispering to him while he rocks.

I take one last second to look over at the other van, now filled with about a dozen women, and think: *Holy shit! They did it.*

At least, I hope one of them is her.

Shaking my head, I jump into the driver's seat, slam the door, and barely wait long enough for one of Enzo's guys to jump in before roaring down the road.

About a block later, a huge kaboom rattles the windows. I take just a moment to glance in the mirror and see the warehouse crumbling into nothing more but rocks and dust.

Re-focusing on the road, I hit the gas, and drive us as quickly to the med bay as I can without getting pulled over.

I swear to God, if Mason dies, I'm going to fucking lose it.

19

~Chloe~

I. Am. Fuming!

These motherfuckers have held me captive in this Goddamn room for at least 8 hours. Maybe more. All I know is that it wasn't dark when they left me with a sandwich and a couple of drinks, and now the sun has been up for an hour.

Fuming.

Absolutely pissed.

How fucking dare they. It's bad enough that they kidnapped me and took me away from my home, my friends, and my job....

Fuck! My job!

Jo must be worried sick. What's it been? Two days now? He must be freaked out since I didn't show up for my shift.

Fuck, fuck, fuck!

I slam my fists into the drywall as hard as I can.

"Stupid, arrogant, smug-ass Bastar-" My rant is cut off by a door slamming somewhere.

My ears twitch as I strain to hear who it may be. Wait, I don't give a shit who it is.

"Assholes! You mother fucking assholes! Let me out. Right. Now!" I punctuate the last two words with a pound of my fist against the door.

Somewhere in the house, I hear low murmurs and press my ear against the door.

"...down. Have to relax...stay there."

I have no idea why they should get to relax while I'm cooped up in this God-forsaken room, so I do what I apparently do best. I scream. I yell. I pound on the door, rattling the hinges with each bang of my fist.

Suddenly, the door swings open. I barely have time to hop back to prevent being whacked in the face.

Gage. Fucking Gage.

His face is beat red, and his scowl is as deep as the sea.

"Calm. The fuck. Down." He spits in a harsh whisper.

Oh, hell no.

I lift my chin, squaring my shoulders, and step right into him.

"No," I sneer in his face. "Let me go, now."

Violence and fury flash in his eyes, but I don't back down.

I won't.

"No. And, before you start, I need your help." With that, he turns away from me, stomping back the way he came.

For a moment, I'm too stunned to move. He left the door open. He asked for help. What the...

Then I vaguely hear him murmur, "Maybe you can talk some sense into Mason."

I stand there for far too long, trying to figure out what in God's name is happening.

Why is he letting me out but not letting me go?

Is this a trick?

And why would he need help with Mason?

After what's probably two minutes of fumbling in confusion, I poke my head out into the hallway. Looking up and down, it looks normal-ish. I mean, cream walls, a couple of doors, and an opening at the end with a bright light from what I assume must be the living room or something.

Toeing out of the door, I quickly surmise there are no personal effects on the walls. No photos, no plaques, nothing.

A male hiss comes from somewhere around the corner.

Blood pumps violently in my ears as I creep closer to the end of the hallway, praying to God I'm not about to end up with a bullet in my head like that man three years ago.

My heart beats in my chest, pounding for a way out, but, like me, it has nowhere to go. Nowhere to hide.

So, I continue forward.

I expect my brain to become one with the wall.

I expect to be attacked violently.

I expect to be tortured mercilessly for whatever crime he feels I've done.

What I don't expect is seeing Mason on the couch, Gage gingerly helping him remove his shirt, and a bright white gauze painted with a bold red center blooming out like a firework.

"Oh my God!" My body moves without my permission, and I rush to Mason's side just as his and Gage's gazes jerk toward me.

"What did you do?" I scream at Gage, fear and anger fighting for dominance in my heart.

He doesn't respond other than to chuff a humorless laugh.

"What makes you think I did anything, Princess?" He sneers low, continuing to work Mason's shirt off of his body.

His toned, delicious, holy fork-nuggets, fine-ass body.

Mason's chuckle, quickly followed by a hiss of pain, brings me out of my shameful ogling.

"Gage didn't do anything, Angel." He grunts. "Just got caught up, is all."

"Caught up? In what? Are they in jail?"

Gage smirks like the dastardly, infuriating man he is, and Mason chuffs a laugh. "No, Angel, they're not."

The look he gives me drains all the blood from my face and I feel it: I feel the tingles, I feel the wooziness, I feel the sway.

I'm just too stunned to do a damn thing about it as my world goes black.

20

~Chloe~

My ears are ringing, and my head is pounding away like a bass drum. *What happened?*

"You passed out." I jump at the familiar raspy timber of Gage's voice coming from next to me.

Shooting up far too quickly, I grab my head and steady myself on the couch. The luxurious, navy blue leather couch. *Good God. Is this thing made from butter?*

Gage and Mason chuckle, causing me to whip my head upward again. I didn't mean to say that out loud.

The events from...however long ago...crash through my mind.

Gage let me out, but he won't let me leave.

They hinted that they had killed someone.

Mason was shot.

"Mason! Oh my God. Are you ok? Why are you standing up?" I quickly shoot to my feet and rush over to him, standing at the far end of the couch.

His smile is not quite as bright as it was the night we first met, and he's a heck of a lot paler.

"I'm ok, Angel. See," He lifts up his shirt to show me the bullet wound that appears to be just to the right of his heart, closer to his shoulder. Then, he quickly turns around, shirt still rucked up, and shows me what can only be described as an exploded exit wound that's been stitched up...well, pretty decently, actually.

Nausea boils in my belly, and I have to force myself to swallow down the bile splashing the back of my throat.

"Wh-what happened?" I whisper, wondering if I even want to know.

Mason sighs, turns to face me with a dopey smile, and lets his shirt fall. "Aw, Angel, are you worried about lil' ol' me?" He flutters his lashes like an idiot, and I swat his opposite arm.

"Seriously. What happened?"

My gaze bounces between his eyes, imploring him to tell me, but he just chews on his lip and nods toward Gage.

Fucking Gage.

I don't want to talk to him.

I don't want to see him.

Hell, I'm not even sure I'm safe standing here.

But curiosity wins out. And he did let me leave the room, so that's something, I suppose.

I slowly swivel to meet Gage's gaze and am immediately drawn in. His presence was always larger than life. He exudes confidence, respect, authority. Now, I'm wondering what signs I missed that he was actually dangerous.

One thing is for sure: Gage has only gotten darker and more delicious since I last saw him. His stubble is more of a statement than a long day, and his deep, brown locks are a little longer on top than they used to be. His icy blue eyes are just as entrancing as they always were, and I find myself unable to look away.

Swallowing the lump in my throat, I ignore what I want to say and continue on the previous line of thought.

"Gage, what happened?"

A muscle ticks in his jaw as he assesses me. For the first time in years, I feel self-conscious and move to cover up, crossing my arms across my body like armor.

His eyes narrow dangerously, and I watch as his broad chest expands, then deflates. Without another word, he turns on his heel and moves to the bar cart at the opposite end of the room.

I watch as he pours himself two fingers of his favorite whiskey, downing it in one gulp. Then he pours another.

"Drink?" He offers as if I'm an actual guest and not a prisoner.

"No, thank you." I annunciate clearly, hoping to convey that I'm not participating in whatever little game he's playing.

He exhales heavily, shaking his head, and mumbles, "Stubborn as always," As he continues to tinker with glasses and drinks on the cart.

A moment later, he turns around and reveals a full glass of a light red liquid and a slice of orange.

"Tequila sunrise, double, just like you like." He walks across the room to offer me the drink. I start to open my mouth to tell him just where he can shove his glass but, Mason beats me to it.

Stepping up behind me, he gently squeezes my shoulders, then leans down and whispers in my ear. "Trust me, Angel. You're going to want a drink for this conversation."

My head turns to face Mason, and I'm once again caught off guard by the gorgeous colors of his hazel eyes and how they make his floppy curls stand out even more. He really is a beautiful man.

But, more than that, I see sincerity and something that looks an awful lot like a plea. A plea for what? I haven't a clue, but I'm guessing I'm about to get way more than I ever bargained for.

21

~Mason~

God, this woman is gorgeous and tough as nails. Not many men are willing to go toe-to-toe with Gage, but she has no problem with it.

Finding out she's Gage's old flame almost killed me.

Finding out she's the Traitor's Princess, well, that part I'm happy to forget about for now... At least until we talk to the Don.

My dick has been at half-mast since she walked into the room. Her eyes went wide with fear and something close to genuine sympathy when she saw my wound. I can't lie, it felt fucking good. Don't get me wrong, it hurts like a bitch. I needed a transfusion, but thankfully, the bullet went all the way through and didn't hit anything vital. So, after I got patched up and had a transfusion and some pain meds, we were on our way back home.

I still can't believe we helped all those women today. I think I heard someone say there were twelve of them. And that one guy, Jenson, was telling his friend that they found their girl.

It was insane, to say the least, and, not for the first time today, I'm struck with the thought that I'd do the same for Chloe. No matter how little I know her or the fact we only had that one night together...

There's just something about her that makes me want to be totally, unequivocally in with her.

Shaking off those thoughts, I return to the conversation.

"Oh my God! So, a bunch of guys rescued a poor girl who was kidnapped by her ex?" She squeaks incredulously.

"Yup." Gage pops the p and takes another swig of his drink.

"And you and some other, what, randos helped?"

She's on her second drink, and I'm not sure she's really ready for the next part.

Gage clears his throat, and leans forward, pressing his elbows into his knees as he rolls the glass tumbler between his hands.

"Not randos, Baby Girl."

"Ah, ah. No *baby girl*. You lost that right."

His eyes narrow into impossibly thin slits; his mouth working back and forth like he's grinding his teeth.

"We'll talk about that later." He starts, then holds up his hand, knowing damn well she's about to interject. "What you're about to learn is a lot, but it's important to the story and to our lives."

He pauses, gauging her reaction. I assume he can see what I see. Fear, anticipation, concern, and a hell of a lot of intrigue.

"Ok." She acquiesces.

With a nod, he really begins. "The men who helped the four other guys are families...." He trails off, letting her have time to absorb each piece of information.

"The head of my family was approached by Enzo, who runs his family."

Her eyes squint as she tries to put the pieces together.

"Ok, so... your what? Dad and Enzo are friends?"

I huff a laugh and groan a little as I lean back against the couch next to her.

"No, Chloe. Mafia families. We are separate families under the umbrella of...

The Italian Mafia."

I lean forward just a bit, wincing from the strain of my newly acquired stitches. A dozen thoughts flash through her eyes until she lands on one...disbelief.

This is punctuated by her abrupt laughter.

Chloe's eyes dance with amusement, and her cheeks pinken beautifully, giving me a brief flashback of another time her cheeks were stained pink.

Curling forward, she slaps her thigh repeatedly, wheezing for breath.

I have to hand it to Gage; he stays completely stoic and seemingly unperturbed by her blatant disbelief of our jobs. Little does she know...

"Oh...my...God... You almost had me, Gage." She sucks in repeated breaths, trying her damndest to get hold of herself, but she's not quite there yet.

"Holy shit...When did you get so funny?!" She yells between additional giggles.

She finally starts to calm down, a few tears draining from her eyes, and she quickly swipes away. "Ok, ok. I'm good."

Clearing her throat, she takes a deep, penetrative breath and fixes her eyes back on Gage.

"Ok, *really:* how do you know Enzo?"

Gage is deathly silent as he tilts his head just so and gazes deep into her eyes.

I squirm quietly, not sure why it's turning me on so much. *Damn, these meds are pretty great.*

But then, I watch as Chloe's face turns from red to a ghastly pale color. Her drink slips from her hand, clattering to the carpet and spilling the remainder of her light-red liquid.

None of us move. I feel like none of us are breathing.

We just sit there, tension building to unprecedented heights as the information truly, completely sinks in.

The moment it clicks, she immediately stands, backing away from Gage, toward the door.

"Holy...shit." She whispers. Her hands are trembling as she continues past me, not allowing either of us to have her back.

"You, you, you-"

"Yes, Angel, we are." I finish softly.

Her eyes ping to mine, and for a whole minute, she's frozen to the spot as she searches my eyes for some kind of relief.

When she finds none, her head tilts, tears begin to stream down her face, and she hunches her shoulders. Her hands come up to her mouth just as she sobs out, "No."

Before I can do or say anything else, she takes off, running toward the door, trying to open the locks with her shaking hands.

When the door doesn't open, she starts banging and screaming out. "Help me! Help! Someone help me!"

I drop my head to the back of the couch with a heavy sigh, knowing she can't get out without the pin but also hating how she's reacting.

Gage exhales heavily and rises to stand. Rolling up his sleeves, showing me a healthy amount of forearm porn, he shoves his hands into his pockets and states, "You can't get out that way, Chloe. And trust me when I say you're safer here."

That gets her attention. She whips around, that fire burning bright in her eyes, and flails her hands in the air while yelling, "Safer how? I've been kidnapped by the fucking Mafia. Oh fuck...Oh my God...are you going to kill me now? Is this because I saw you kill a man at the ice cream shop? I didn't tell anyone. I swear. I won't tell. Please. Please let me go."

She's spiraling completely out of control. Her whole body starts trembling just before she hits the ground, knees first. A sob rips out of her chest, and I can't help it; I push myself up, grunting from the movement, then toe over to her.

"Please, Angel. Please calm down." I coo softly. Her cries hit a fever pitch, and she sounds like she's moments away from puking from the force. Dropping to the ground, I wrap my arms around her, not worrying about the pain, and hold her to me.

I hear her desperate pleas, and my heart breaks for her.

Wait until she finds out the rest...

Fifteen minutes later, Gage and I have finally convinced her that neither of us, nor the Don, is after her: that she's not here for us to kill.

She's just about finished with her bottle of water when she looks up at me with glassy eyes. A whole storm of emotions filters through them as she bites her beautifully plump lip. Then she turns to Gage.

I hear her swallow audibly, then inhales a deep, restorative breath. "So... the Mafia?" She clears her throat, runs a hand through her now kinda greasy hair, and sighs.

Gage leans back against his chair and fiddles with his still-empty tumbler. "Yes, Chloe. But we only want to keep you safe. That's all I've ever wanted."

His sincerity hits me square in the gut, and I have to force down the snap reaction to go and pee on her leg.

It's that thought that makes me realize I've got it bad, and this is really going to hurt if she walks away.

2 2

~Gage~

Chloe has handled this whole conversation much better than I figured she would. Unfortunately for her, it isn't over yet.

I study her for a moment, relishing in the familiar memories of her laughter, her smile, her all-around brightness in my dark world. She's grown as a woman, and is definitely more confident in her body, and I feel more drawn to her than ever.

Flicking my eyes toward Mason, I see he's already head-over-ass for her. Not that I can blame him. But we're nowhere near ready to start anything again.

I inhale deeply, then push the breath from my lungs as I look over at her. "Chlo...there's more."

I keep my voice steady, and firm, but hopefully inject just enough sincerity that she continues to hear us, understand us, and doesn't totally break.

Although, if she does, we'll be there to put the pieces back together. *If she lets us.*

She groans and throws her body backward against the couch, covering her eyes with her arm. After a beat of silence, she flails her free arm in the air in a "Get on with it" motion.

Connecting my gaze with Mason's, I silently convey that this part will be hard for her, and he should be ready. Thankfully, we're on the same page. His jaw tightens, and he gives a singular nod and moves his gaze back to Chloe.

"Chloe, you're more important than you may realize. That guy in the parking lot, he's not the only one after you."

She sits up slowly, methodically, as if her brain can't process the information and move at the same time.

"Why would people be after me?" The gasp that leaves her the moment she voices her question tells me she's making her own connections. "Is it because we were together? I'm a target because I was with you?" She cries incredulously, rolling her eyes as she stands, and abruptly starts pacing.

She begins muttering incoherently under her breath, and I can feel her spinning out of control. Standing slowly, I step toward her and brush a hand down her arm. She flinches from my touch, meeting my gaze with fire in her eyes. "You did this!" She screams while pointing a finger in my face.

I can't help it, I smirk. That damn fire is so hot and one of the reasons I've always loved her. *I mean, used to love her.*

My smirk doesn't fade as I gently push her hand away from my face and meet her stare for stare. "Chloe," I say low enough for only her to hear. "You were a target far before I came along."
I wait as she processes the information. Once her brows furrow and her head tilts, I drop the bomb.

"Your father was the Don of a very powerful family. But, he turned rat. Then, he put your mother into The Program before doing the same for himself."

She's utterly still and completely silent as I begin to tear what she thought she knew to shreds.

With a gentle squeeze, I move back and plant myself in my chair. Keeping my eyes on hers, I continue. "When your mother died, that was a hit from another family. They're trying to get him to climb out of hiding, and the best way to do that is,"

"To go after his family." She finishes in disbelief.

Her throat moves with a heavy swallow as she stares deep into my eyes, probably hoping for a punchline. Unfortunately, there isn't one.

Abruptly, she stands, crosses to the far side of the living room, and begins pacing while wringing her fingers.

"So, I had a dad, a real one. But he was a narc, right?" She pauses long enough to catch Mason's gaze. Once he nods in confirmation, she resumes pacing.

"And he put Mom and me into witness protection, then went into it himself separately. But why?"

She's still pacing, so I try to keep my tone calm and firm, even though all I want to do is go to her, comfort her, hold her.

"There are people everywhere with facial recognition and all sorts of other hacking abilities. Some within the Italian families and a lot in others, like the Bratva." I spit at the thought of them getting their hands on her.

Another moment is spent in silence as she chews over my words.

Her pacing begins to slow; her teeth graze across her deliciously plump lip as she comes to a stand before me. Her chest heaves with a stuttered breath just as her eyes flutter open to meet my gaze. The tears forming tell me exactly what she's about to ask next.

"And I was a job...for you."

The implication is clear: The hurt is written all over her face, but I don't move. I know trying to comfort her would be futile at best and destructive at worst.

Instead, I take an ice cube from my tumbler and clink it against my teeth, relishing in the cold bite as I crunch into it. Her eyes are transfixed on my mouth, which is exactly what I was hoping for.

As her pupils begin to dilate, I run a tongue over my bottom lip and have to stop myself from groaning as her eyes follow.

That's when I divulge my greatest secret.

"Yes, Baby Girl, I was assigned to watch after you, to follow you, to learn all I could about you in case you had any idea where you're traitor of a father is."

I pause, letting her feel the weight of my words before rising to stand in front of her. Like that spit-fire she is, she doesn't flinch back, she doesn't cower. Instead, she lifts her chin and meets my gaze, a storm brewing in her ocean eyes.

"Don wants your father to pay. Not you. He's a man who's done many bad things, but children are always innocent in his mind. So, yes, you started as a job. And then," I stick my hands in my pants and shrug, my gaze flicking quickly to Mason, who's watching on with more fascination than I could have ever imagined.

"And then..." My eyes snap back to Chloe, and I see the hurt mixed with hope, the fear mixed with fight. I can't help the small smile that forms across my face.

"And then, *Chloe,* I fell in love with you."

My voice drops until it's just above a whisper, just loud enough for her and Mason to hear in the otherwise quiet room. "And I never stopped."

A whirlwind of emotion flashes through her eyes. Another breath passes before she jumps into my arms; wrapping herself around me and delivering a punishing kiss.

My heart beats in my throat as I feel redemption, punishment, love, and anger roll from her mouth to mine. It's cathartic and terrifying.

But it's everything I never hoped to wish for again.

Knowing now isn't the time to get too lost in each other, I break the kiss. Our panting breaths mingle, pupils are blown wide, and both of our cheeks heated with passion.

Acting on pure instinct, I lean in and kiss her forehead, pressing her tightly against me; scared to let her go, scared to open myself up again, just plain scared.

But, I have to, we have to, or we'll never be able to truly live in peace together.

And that's all I truly want.

<h1 style="text-align:center">23</h1>

<h1 style="text-align:center">~Chloe~</h1>

Holy shit! Kissing Gage was everything I remembered and so much more. I've been running for years, and for what?

He lets me go with another peck to my lips, and I swear I feel it sizzle in my panties. But there'll be time for that later. Right now, we need to hash some things out. Like, where does Mason fit in with all of this?

Oh shit! Mason!

I quickly turn to find Mason leaning back in his chair, a cocky grin playing across his face. "Don't mind me, that was hot," He groans as he not-so-subtly adjusts himself.

I giggle out because he's so damn silly, but quickly push it down when I see his eyes flash with lust.

"Um, so…" I trail off, not sure how to even approach the subject.

"Let's save that for now, Baby Girl." Gage chuckles. "We'll have plenty of time to talk about that later. For now, I need to know…"

In a move too quick for me to comprehend, he slides his arms around me, pressing my back to his chest, and brings me down into his chair with him so I'm sitting firmly in his lap.

Like a mature, confident woman, I giggle like a schoolgirl.

Sheesh. How he makes me feel clearly hasn't diminished at all.

Once we're both comfortable, he turns me so I can look down into those mesmerizing, clear, blue eyes. "Chloe," He begins with a choked-off sound. "Why did you run?"

Ice floods my veins as the memories come pouring into me. Only, this time, it's not fear I'm feeling, it's confusion, it's mourning, it's...something quite sad.

I take a deep breath, sweep a lock of his hair away from his eyes, and furrow my brows as my eyes bounce between his.

"The night I got this tattoo..." I begin, raising up my left forearm to show off the beautiful semi-colon butterfly and cross. "When I was finished, you were gone. So, I walked over to the custard shop."

Understanding filters through his gaze, and his mouth forms into a stern, straight line. Before he can say anything else, I continue. "I was so scared, Gage. I had no idea you were capable of that. And then I thought, maybe I didn't know you at all..."

I choke on a sob as the sheer terror I felt that night overwhelms my heart and soul.

Gage wraps his arms tighter around me, allowing me to bury my head into his neck while I cry for the little girl I was and the clueless woman I still am.

As he strokes my hair, I feel him start to slowly sway our bodies in the chair. "Chloe, the man that night, and the one from the other night were sent by the *Bratva*. There's a huge reward for capturing you."

For some reason, that sends a jolt of fire through my body. "What?!" I screech incredulously. "Stuff like that really happens? Someone put out a hit on me??"

I'm squawking like a bird but holy crap! How is this my life? "Yes, Chloe. Stuff like that is very real. But I've been there every step of the way, protecting you." He states.

"At least until you ran away."

He doesn't say anything else. He doesn't admonish me; he doesn't chastise me. He just holds me and allows me to think about the last thirty minutes of my life—hell, the last four years of my life.

After a few minutes of nothing more than our breathing to fill the soothing silence, I stutter in a deep breath. Leaning up, I look at Gage right in his eyes, hold his face in my hands, and vow, "I will never leave again. If you still want this, want me; I'm all yours."

I gently kiss his full lips, hoping to pour every ounce of love and forgiveness into them. When he breaks the kiss, he heaves a heavy sigh, bites his lip, and looks over at Mason.

"Before you say that, you need to know something else."

His eyes meet Mason's from across the room, and I glance between them repeatedly. Then it finally hits me. "Oh my God! You two are together. Mason! I'm so sorry! I never would have..." I mumble incoherently as I practically fall out of Gage's lap and rush over to Mason. "I'm so sorry. That was so rude of me. Please forgive me."

Crouching low next to his chair, I implore him to believe me. I would never knowingly come between anybody who's in a relationship. No matter what.

But there's a lightness to his eyes, even though it looks like he's trying desperately to hold onto his stern scowl.

Suddenly, he bursts into a fit of laughter, bends down, and scoops me into his lap. His wince of pain is the only thing that gives away his injury, but he ignores it. "Angel, stop, you're fine. Yes, Gage and I are... together." He looks over at Gage with the sexiest, smuggest grin I've ever seen.

Some kind of silent conversation passes between them. After a long, tense, silence, he finally looks back at me. "But, Gage and I like to share. We share each other, and, on occasion, we share women."

Brain offline

I feel myself blink.

I think I'm breathing, but I'm not totally sure.

What did he just say?

His rich, throaty chuckle vibrates through my body, and my brain short-circuits again. *These men are going to kill me.*

My eyes grow as wide as saucers as I blink up at him. I'm pretty sure I look like a baby owl with how wide they have grown.

Then, I look over at Gage, who is now sporting a wide-legged stance with one arm resting behind the chair he's using as his throne.

"I'm sorry...wh-what?"

Gage grins and rubs his bottom lip in that stupidly sexy way that men do right as his head tilts. "Instead of telling you, how about we show you?"

And now I'm goo, on the floor, that they're going to have to mop up because- *pardon your finest fuck?- How did we even get here?*

Mason maneuvers me until I'm sitting on his lap, my back to his chiseled chest and his huge dick poking my ass through his sweats.

He gives me a gentle kiss right below my ear and whispers, "Come on, Angel. It'll be fun. And if you ever want to stop, you have your safeword, right?" He growls low in his chest just before pulling my earlobe into his mouth and sucking my earring right off. My panties incinerate on the spot, and I'm all too aware that I haven't showered since arriving here.

"Um, can I, can I shower first?" I squeak as I clamber away from his lap quickly.

Their collective chuckles follow me through the living room until I hear Gage call out, "First door on the left, Baby Girl. And don't keep us waiting too long. You're perfectly delicious just as you are."

Mason's answering groan follows me down the hallway. They both begin murmuring to each other but I don't pause to listen. Instead, I hook the first left and slam the door behind me, locking it quickly with a *schnick*, before immediately backing into the sink cabinet and damn near falling to the floor.

What type of alternate universe have I found myself in, and why do I want what they're offering so badly?

24

~Chloe~

My whole body tingles with anticipation. I may or may not have rummaged through the cabinets and found a bag of disposable razors to help with my prickly problem. Then, I scrubbed every centimeter of my body, even though the only items in the shower were a heavenly, yet manly, mix of eucalyptus and leather.

It's both erotic and overwhelming using their products as I continue to figure out if I'm really going to go through with this.

Gage and I used to talk about adding a third into our scenes, but neither of us could really handle sharing. Would it be just in the bedroom? I mean, how does this work? They're a couple. Would I just be the girl they fuck?

Can I be that for Gage? For the man I once loved more than life itself?

Tip-toeing out of the room, wearing one of their long-sleeved button-up shirts- sleeves rolled past my elbows- I bite a hole in my lip as I quietly make my way down the hallway until I can peer just around the corner.

What I see causes the briefs I borrowed to immediately grow wet with my arousal.

Gage is still spread out in his chair, but now his pants are off, his bare legs and feet framing Mason's perfectly naked back. And oh, holy shit. The muscles in his back move and twitch with delight as his head bobs up and down in Gage's lap.

Oh, Oh!!!

My eyes widen, and I may or may not moan at the perfectly naughty display in front of me.

Judging by the twitch of Gage's quads and the sudden stillness of Mason's back, I did, in fact, moan out.

"Come here, Baby Girl." Gage moans at something that Mason is doing, and, dammit, I'm curious. Far too curious to just stand here and watch from afar.

Nope, I want to be right up where the action is.

Based on the slurping sounds and Mason's head bobbing, he's attacking Gage's cock again. *Why is that so hot?*
My heart rate doubles as I approach with soft feet. The scene in front of me unfolds as I get closer and watch in fascination as Gage throws his head back on a grunt, moving his hands to the sides of Mason's head, and begins fucking up into his mouth.

"Good boy, that's my good little boy. You're doing such a good job showing Chloe how good you can be."

Mason groans deep in his throat, just like I remember Gage used to love, and I watch with rapt attention as the veins in his forearms jump.

Gage tilts his head up and looks down at Mason, using his thumbs to wipe away the tears leaking from Mason's eyes. The look, the motion, the moment is so damn sweet, so damn gentle, that it hits me square in the heart.

I'm the outsider. They're happy together. They're good together. *And who the hell am I?*

Emotion clogs my throat, and I realize that this is all a mistake. I can't be a third wheel in this obviously true, loving relationship. I don't say anything. I don't make a sound; I just turn on my heel and flee to my room.

As I hit the hall, I could hear grunts and whispers right before Mason calls out to me.

Tonight was too much. This is too much. I just need to go to bed, and then I can figure out a living situation.

No, I'm not going back home to be 'Grace.' I'm a wreck, not stupid. But I can't stay *here*. Not with the man I used to love more than anything in this world, and not with a man I've imagined having more with. It's too complicated, and if I let this happen, I'd be the one shattered in the end.

Slamming the door shut, I hit the lights off and jump into bed. Squeezing my eyes shut, I start counting backward from 100, praying that I can go to sleep and forget this whole day.

No dice.

The moment I hit ninety-four, I hear my door creak open, the light from the hall brightening the world beyond my eyelids.

"I can't do this," I whisper. "Please, just go. I'm not going anywhere tonight. Just; please go."

I keep my eyes closed, not wanting to see the looks they are probably giving me.

A shadow crosses in front of my eyelids, but I don't open them. Instead, I lie as still as possible as the smell of eucalyptus envelops my senses. "Tomorrow, Baby girl. We'll talk tomorrow. Please don't let that little voice in your head lie to you. We want you, more than a night... and more than your body." He leans in, presses a chaste kiss to my forehead, and backs away.

Gage must now be near the door when he murmurs, almost too low for me to hear. "I still love you, Chloe. I never stopped."

And with that, he closes the door, plummeting me into pure darkness.

25

~Mason~

To say I'm disappointed by tonight's outcome seems like an understatement. Not that I only see Chloe as a sexual object but, she's a badass; one that I can't fucking get enough of.

She had a whole shitload of information dumped on her and still held her head high, still got aroused, and still had the audacity to keep living instead of burying her hand in the sand and hoping the problem goes away.

I pad back to our room while Gage checks on Chloe so I can hop in our oversized shower. Clicking on the Bluetooth speaker attached to the shower wall, I slide my phone from my pocket and thumb over to YouTube Music, needing something to calm the confusion swirling through my mind.

It's one thing to have blue-balls, it's another thing entirely to be so twisted up over a woman that I've only been with for a month; that I already know I want to spend forever with.

Human by Rag'n'Bone Man begins to play as I strip down and throw my dingy, bloodied clothing into the nearby hamper. I hiss out in pain from the movement, but I'm thankful the bullet went all the way through, but it really does hurt like a bitch.

A door creaks open, and Gage steps into view through the sliding glass door. "Hey, Baby Boy." He murmurs with a grin. "You ok?" His question is conversational enough, but I know that he probably thinks I'm upset that I didn't get to finish him. Or that he left me behind to check on Chloe. Or...

"Stop, Baby. I can hear you freaking out from here." His gentle touch causes me to flinch, not having realized that he's not only naked but is now in the shower with me.

His hands find the sides of my face, thumbs stroking up and down my jawline. "I don't say this enough, but Mason, I love you. You brought light into my darkness; you see me, and I see you. Chloe is not a replacement for you. Ever. Whether she joins us or decides she can't handle this, it's you and I. Forever."

With that, he leans in and captures my lips with his, swiping my bottom lip with his tongue. I don't even have time to acquiesce as he surges forward and forces his hard tongue into my mouth. I groan out as he plunders my mouth with his dominance, and all rational thought flies out of my head.

This kiss, his kiss, is hot and loving and the absolute best of Gage.

My body melts into his embrace, and I wrap my arms around his wide shoulders. His thick, calloused hand finds my hard cock between our bodies, and he gives a healthy squeeze, pumping upward once.

A long hiss escapes through my teeth when his blunt thumb swipes the slit in my tip, rubbing the bead of pre-cum around the head before plunging his hand back down my length.

The water adds just enough lubrication that he slides down and back up my throbbing cock with ease; squeezing just enough that I ride the perfect edge of pain versus pleasure.

Gage breaks our kiss, panting out a groan, then leans back and spits directly on my dick. It's so deliciously filthy that I almost explode right then and there.

But then, he surprises me. The man falls to his knees before me!

Water pelts down from the spray and drips off his lashes as he stares up at me. "Baby Boy, Mason, you are my everything. And that is something that will never change."

With a sweeter-than-candy smile, he leans down and takes my entire length into his mouth, trailing his tongue down the thick vein pulsing underneath my shaft.

A low, growling groan echoes up through my chest, and I slam my head back against the tiles. He sucks in his cheeks and slurps his way back to my tip, swirling his tongue around the crown, then plunges back down my throbbing cock. When the tip of my dick hits the back of his throat, he gags a little but breathes through it fantastically.

Gage's head begins to bounce up and down on my cock, and I have to forcefully peel my eyes open to look down on this perfect, beautiful man that I call mine.

My heart pounds deep in my chest as I take him in. I watch, transfixed, at this larger-than-life, dominant man on his knees for me. No, it's not the first time he's sucked me off, but it's usually in a scene with me tied up in some fashion.

And he's never gone to his knees.

This...this means everything. He means everything.

Water droplets fall from his lashes as he bores into my gaze, bobbing, slurping, grunting around my cock. His lips turn up on the sides in a gentle smile just before he grips my thighs and brings my hips forward, fucking his mouth on my cock.

The sensations, the emotions, everything from the past few days, heck, the past few years, boils down to this moment.

The moment he fully commits himself to *me* and shows me with his actions that I'm his, and he's mine.

With that realization, a galaxy of stars burst through my eyes as my balls draw up and unload into his hot, waiting mouth. It takes him a minute to swallow it all, but, dammit, he does, and I think I fall even more in love with this man.

Reaching down, I palm the back of his neck and pull him up to me. Our breaths mingle in harsh pants for mere seconds before I slam my lips to his, relishing how we taste together.

The kiss is hot, blazing in fact, and over quickly as there's something I really need to say.

"I love you, Gage. I always have."

My eyes bounce between his as the word creates a symphony around us.

I grapple for breath as he raises his hand to cup my cheek. Rubbing his thumb across my jaw, his eyes are alight with too many emotions to decipher.

Until they shine with one.

"I love you, Mason. My past, my present, my future are all yours." Then he slams his lips to mine in a dominating kiss, rightfully claiming his position in this relationship, and causing my heart to swell with more love than I have felt from anyone.

26

~Chloe~

Morning sunlight streams through the lone window, and the heavenly smell of coffee wafts through the halls into my room.

With a groan, I flip to my other side, away from the bright sun, and blearily open my eyes to find...nothing.

Oh, yeah. I'm at the guys' house. And this room is bare as fuck.

The events of last night rush through me in a slideshow of fucked-up proportions. But it's only one that I latch onto: the visions of Mason enthusiastically going down on Gage moments before I chickened out on joining them, too afraid to come between what the two of them clearly have.

Rubbing the sleep from my eyes, I throw my blanket off and swing my legs over the side of the bed. I pull my arms behind me, interlacing my fingers, and stretch my chest and back until I feel every muscle loosen.

Slipping from the bed, I pad toward the door and pray to God they didn't lock me in again.

I blow out a breath of relief when the handle gives way, allowing me to pull the door wide open.

Poking my head out, I check the hall, then beeline to the bathroom, my bladder protesting every step of the way.

After handling my business and washing my hands, I meander down the hall, following the scent of liquid gold and I'm struck once again with how sparsely decorated this place is. Or at least the room I'm in and the hallway.

As I enter the living room, I take a moment to really take it in. Yesterday was a hodge-podge of information overload, so I wasn't necessarily concerned with my surroundings, just the men in the room with me.

There's a giant, at least 70-inch, TV on a thin, black TV stand. Two black bookshelves frame each side and are littered with books of all shapes, sizes, and colors.

I run my fingers along a row of spines and quirk my lips as I see some of them are romance novels.

I wonder who those belong to.

Humming to myself, I continue my perusal until I encounter a multi-shelf section of classic literature. Everything from Pride and Prejudice to a beautiful copy of Alice's Adventures in Wonderland, complete with a multitude of other Lewis Carroll works.

My smile grows wider as I slip the giant, light blue book off the shelf and thumb through the silver-lined pages. This book is, without a doubt, my favorite classic tale of all time. I even like the Tim Burton movie versions.

A throat clearing behind me causes me to startle, and I almost drop the precious book. Thankfully, I recovered quickly and slid it back to its rightful place.

Turning around, I see Mason standing there in nothing but a pair of dark grey sweats, and I choke on my tongue. This man is positively delicious. All lean muscles, porn-worthy forearms, and a killer Adonis belt. *No pun intended.*

His chortle brings me out of my shameless perusal, and he holds out a steaming mug of what I assume is coffee. "Thought you could use some caffeine. I know that last night was a lot so...yeah."

With a self-deprecating grin, he thrusts the mug closer to me, and I take it with shaky hands. Reminders of last night punch a shock through my system as I grasp onto the mug like a lifeline.

My hands tremble as I lift the mug to my lips and take a long, sweet sip. The moan that rips through my throat is indecent but I can't help it, this coffee is perfection.

I feel my shoulders begin to drop, the kinks in my back begin to unravel, and I slowly make my ascent back to the land of the living.

Fluttering my eyes back open, I find Mason boring into my very soul with the sweetest damn smile I've ever seen. And, just like that, I relax a little more.

"Thank you," I whisper with a shy smile. "And, thank you for letting me stay here but, maybe we should talk about finding me a place of my own."

His face immediately transforms into a deep scowl, and I gasp at how terrifying it looks.

"No." Is all he says, turning on his heel and damn near stomping away.

I can't lie, it takes far too long for my brain to recover from the emotional whiplash but, thankfully, I do; just in time to chase him into the kitchen.

"What do you mean "No"?" I scream out, slamming my mug onto the beautiful white marble countertop.

The sexy backside of this infuriating man ignores me and taunts me with each flex and jump as he rummages around in the black stainless steel refrigerator.

"I mean what I say, and Gage will agree. No, you may not move out. Not right now."

He punctuates his statement with a kick of the door closed and begins to drop the contents in his arms.

A carton of eggs, milk, cheese, bell peppers, and mushrooms forms a pile right in the middle of the island as he angrily snaps the black wooden cabinets open, brandishing a large frying pan, a spatula, and salt and pepper in seconds.

"Pardon me, but last I checked, this was my life. You can't just go around kidnapping people, Mason!"

With a roar, he whips away from the stove and marches toward me. I don't flinch because, somewhere deep inside my heart, I know this man would never hurt me.

"We can if someone's trying to kill you or sell you off to the highest bidder, Chloe." He spits my name like I'm being a petulant child.

"What the hell are you talking about? I'm a big girl; I can handle myself."

Now, he's chest-to-chest with me. I have to strain my neck so I can look up at him and see that he is fuming.

His nostrils flare with each inhale, and his face is contorted in a deep, red mask of rage.

I expect him to yell some more, but, instead, he grits his teeth and pushes out, "There are worse things than death, Chloe. Ask the women we saved last night."

Well, shit...

I won't say he's right, but there are signs.

I reach up, wrapping my hands around his neck, and kiss him fiercely, pouring every ounce of rage and fear that I have coursing through my body.

He groans deep in his throat, then swipes everything off of the island next to us, leaning down and picking me up by my ass, and slamming me onto the countertop.

Fever runs rampant through my body as he dives back into the kiss, licking the seam of my mouth before plunging his tongue inside. He fucks my mouth in a similar way that he fucked me a week ago. And damn if it doesn't soak my borrowed boxers thoroughly.

I moan as his hands deftly strip the sweatpants- that were sweetly lying next to me on the bed- right off my legs. He wastes no time ripping the boxers away from my body, leaving me officially bare in front of him; squishy thighs and all.

His lips smash onto mine again as he rushes to free his hard cock, already tenting his pants.

After another groan, he breaks the kiss and steps back. My mouth greedily follows him, and I whimper with the loss of his warmth, of his touch.

Someone clears their throat to my right, and my eyes fly open as I snap my head in that direction. Standing there, in nothing more than a pair of deliciously tight red boxer briefs, is Gage.

The tattoos that mark his body make him look like I imagine my book boyfriends do; mysterious, edgy, fucking hot!

His deep, throaty chuckle brings me out of my daze, and I realize too late that I was blatantly staring at his still impressive package.

"See something you like, Angel?" I jump as Mason's mouth finds my neck and begins planting teasing, open-mouth kisses along my beating pulse point. When he sticks his tongue out and licks a path from the bottom of my neck all the way to my earlobe, I groan out, trying and failing to close my legs as his large, thin fingers grip me above my knees and hold me wide.

"Don't be shy, Angel. Let us show you how great we can be together."

My mind is already going hazy as Gage's eyes turn from hungry to downright ravenous. He has his Dom eyes, and my body clearly remembers as I begin my ascent into sub-space.

Mason bites down on my earlobe, flicking it back and forth, and I moan out a breathy, "Yes, p-please."

I'm already panting, my chest heaving and my nipples peeking beneath the shirt I borrowed.

"What's your safeword, Baby Girl?" Gage asks, sounding just a little breathless himself.

"Pink, ah, Pink Unicorn." I cry out when Mason's fingers connect with my clit, rubbing tender, slow circles around my needy bud.

"Good girl." He pants out, then moves in to dominate my mouth again.

Before I can even move to wrap around him, Gage commands. "Baby Boy, recliner."

Mason and I break away, and he gives me the dopiest, most adorable grin. His eyes are blown wide and gazed over, and that's when I know he's headed off to sub-space, too.

Oh fuck, this is going to be so damn hot.

"Yes, sir." He grunts out, yanking up his sweats and walking toward Gage. As he goes to step around, Gage grabs him by the throat, and I watch in fascination as Mason's whole body damn near drops in submission.

"Make this good for her, and I'll make it good for you," Gage says just above a whisper. Then he grabs him by the throat, hauls him closer, and mashes his lips to Mason's. Watching the two men basically tongue-fuck each other is phenomenally erotic, and I begin squirming on the cool countertop, knowing better than to touch myself but really, really wanting to.

Just as I whimper, my arousal making a small puddle beneath me, Gage breaks the connection and nods at Mason. Then he steals one last fleeting kiss.

Stepping away, Mason swaggers into the living room, leaving Gage and me alone.

27

~Gage~

I woke up hard. I came to the kitchen hard. And then, these two little brats were moments away from fucking on my countertop. And now, I'm painfully hard. So hard I wouldn't flinch if my dick tore a hole right through my briefs.

I wasn't sure Chloe would be willing to play, especially since they were yelling at each other moments before but, hot damn, she looks more than ready. Her chest is heaving, her nipples are tiny, little points straining through the shirt, and I can see her squirming as she rubs her thighs together.

Yeah, I've got it bad. But, so does she.

Her eyes went from lust-filled to submissive so damn fast that I almost blew my load standing there. Thankfully, I've practiced restraint religiously, so it's a little easier to hold off. A little.

The past few days have felt like a fucked up dream; one I didn't want to wake from. But, seeing her and Mason here together brought the reality, our reality, to life. Now I'm hoping I don't wake up to find it gone; like I did three years ago.

I just don't think my heart can take it again.

Chloe whimpers, snapping me out of my trance, and I prowl toward her. Ready to make her feel everything I have felt for three years.

Yes, I know she was scared, but dammit, she should have said something, anything. Instead, she disappeared.

New name, new life, new *boyfriends*.

A growl rumbles in my chest as I come to stand in front of her. My hand reaches up and grasps the back of her neck, lifting her gaze to meet mine. "Mine," I grunt, forcing her to see every emotion: the good, the bad, the downright ugly.

Swallowing heavily, I look deep into her hooded eyes and muster up the apology she deserves. "Chloe, I'm so sorry. I hid so many things from you. Yes, it was for my job, but I swear to you, my feelings were and are as real as I am standing before you. I know it was a shock, and I know I hurt you but, I swear, I would never hurt you on purpose. You are mine, Chloe Rossi, just as I am yours."

Her eyes begin to fill with tears as her gaze softens. Looking between my eyes she leans her head toward mine, meeting her forehead with mine.

"Yours," She whispers.

And then, she's kissing me.

Her sweet flavor, vanilla mixed with coffee, envelopes my senses and damn near knocks me on my ass.

Moving off of her neck, my arms meet below her hips as I grasp onto her deliciously round ass. She already knows where I'm going with this as she wraps her legs around mine, forcing her wet heat to squish against my raging hard-on. Without another thought, I lift her off the counter and walk with her, securely in my arms, into the living room.

Only when I reach Mason's chair do I break our kiss, allowing both of us the breath of air we need.

Her eyes are glazed and floaty, telling me she's seconds from subspace. With a smirk, I gently release her, pushing her against me just hard enough that she feels my cock as she slides down my body to stand in front of me.

I glance at Mason and see him fantastically naked, sitting in his chair like it's a throne, as his cock juts proudly away from his body.

His eyes meet mine and I'm almost knocked back by the raw vulnerability, the pure desire I see there. With a nod, I clear my throat and step back, allowing my Dom persona to wash over me.

"Baby Girl, shirt off. Baby Boy, hands behind your head. No touching."

Chloe hesitates for only half a beat before ripping her shirt up and over her head. Her tits are gloriously bare and I salivate at the overwhelming need to put them in my mouth.

But that will have to wait.

"Present," I say to Chloe as I take one large step back.

Like the good girl she always has been, she immediately falls to her knees, ass in the air, and arms reaching above her head on the floor. It's kind of like Child's Pose in Yoga... minus the clothes.

Mason groans as he gets the perfect view of her delectable ass and her soaking pussy. His hands stay behind his head, but based on the flash of hunger in his eyes and the way his muscles have gone taut, I know that I'm winding him up in just the right way.

Stepping around her, I inspect her from all sides in complete silence. Her harsh breaths lift from the floor, and I can see her pussy clenching with need. *She always felt overly vulnerable in this position.*

But it was this position that caused her to bring down her barriers with me the first time. It's only fitting that we start over with the same amount of vulnerability.

All of us.

The longer I stand there, the closer she gets to subspace. Needing to feel her, needing to touch her right this second, I say, "You were a naughty girl."

She doesn't respond, as I knew she wouldn't, so I continue on.

"You left me without a backward glance. Threw everything away because of a fleeting moment. One you should have come to me about."

I bring my hand down on her ass, just enough to cause her to yelp, then slide my palm down the now-warm patch of skin.

"I-I'm sorry." She whimpers out.

"You're sorry. Hhhmmmm. I don't know. I still think I owe you more punishment. Say, one swat for every year?"

That's way below the mark, but, honestly, I don't really want to punish her. Not today. I want to ravish her.

But, still, she needs to learn. She needs to come to me, come to Mason when something is wrong or broken. I won't survive losing her again, and, based on how Mason looks at her, he won't survive losing her at all.

"Y-Yes, sir. I'm sorry, sir."

"Ok. Three more, and you're going to count. Don't move, or I'll add to it."

Her whole body trembles as I rear back with my hand and pop the other ass cheek. *Damn, she has the perfect size for a whole handprint.*

"One!" She screams just as I bring my hand back down on the other side. "Two!"

"Good girl, one more, and then you can sit in Mason's lap. Would you like that, Baby girl?"

Her body is wracked with tremors as she shakily exhales a hissed, "Yes, s-sir."

With a smug grin, I look over at Mason to see his eyes are wide and unfocused, and the tip of his dick is almost purple-like: the barbells of his magic cross piercing standing out against the angry appendage.

Turning around, I quickly whap her ass cheek again and immediately begin soothing my hand over both, simultaneously taking out the sting while also just grazing her pussy lips with my fingertips.

"Th-three!" She moans out loud, thrusting her ass into my hand.

"Oh, you did so well, Baby Girl," I coo as I dip my fingers near her entrance and scoop up some of the juices flowing from her body.

Sticking my hand up and behind me, I order, "Taste her."

Mason immediately leans up, grasps hold of my wrist, and twirls his tongue around my fingers. A filthy groan escapes me, and my dick punches my briefs.

"Good b-boy." I hiss as he begins tongue-fucking my fingers like he would my aching cock.

He releases me with a satisfied *pop* and immediately leans back in the recliner, fisting the arms with white-knuckled grips.

Chloe moans in response, her body vibrating with desire but staying otherwise still.

"Such a good girl," I whisper, brushing the hair off her neck and draping it over her left shoulder.

Leaning over her, I position my fingers at her entrance, just outside so she can feel my heat, and whisper, "Does my girl need a reward?" She mewls in response, her head falling and thumping to the floor as she moans breathlessly, "Please."

I chuckle in response and dip my fingertips in; two fingers for my two loves. Her pussy clenches the tips so tightly that it's all I can do not to replace them with my dick. But I don't. Tonight isn't about me, or Mason, or even her. It's about all of us connecting, all of us being vulnerable, all of us being in.

I feel a gush of wetness just as I start to slowly pump my fingers in and out of her perfectly hot channel. Her body responds just as beautifully as I remember as it grips my fingers with each pass, desperate to keep me inside.

"Mason, our girl is soaked. I think she's already ready for you." Mason chuckles when Chloe freezes, and I can't help but prod. "No? You don't want Mason's thick, pierced cock fucking up into the pussy while I lick you to orgasm?"

Both of them groan out, and Chloe begins fucking herself with my fingers. Her juices slide down my wrist, and I'd bet there's already a puddle forming on the floor.

"Yesss. Please. Oh, please let me come. Please." She thrashes her head side-to-side as I up my tempo, curling my fingers around to hit that magic spot at her front wall.

"Did you hear that, Baby Boy? Our girl wants to cum. Should we let her?"

"Oh fuck, yes, please, Sir. Let her cum." He whines just as his hips thrust forward into nothing, so hopped up on the scene unfolding but knowing better than to do anything without permission.

"Hear that, Chloe baby? Mason said you can come."

We're rewarded with a deep, guttural groan as I reach my free hand underneath her and attack her clit like I know she likes it. My girl needs an almost vibrating pressure but not so hard that it pushes in; just enough that she gets the constant feeling of movement.

"Cum, for me, Baby Girl. Come for Mason so he can fuck this sweet pussy like a Good Boy."

And that does it.

She goes off like a bottle rocket. Her pussy clenches around my fingers as I continue to ruin her clit. Her scream echoes around the room as her body continues riding my fingers almost mindlessly.

As her orgasm subsides, I remove the pressure from her clit and lazily pump in and out a few times, twisting and scissoring my fingers to prepare her for his girthy beast.

With a final whimper, her body melts into the ground, causing Mason and I to chuckle. Turning, I lock gazes with him and see everything I could have ever wanted in his eyes: acceptance, peace, love, and desire. It's all right there, and I know, now more than ever, that this is exactly where we're all supposed to be.

28

~Chloe~

I. Am. Goo. Boneless, personless, indecipherable goo. My head is fuzzy and floaty, and I swear it's better than any drug.

Chuckles barely breech the fog, but I'm far too blissed out to care. That is until I hear his whiskey-butter voice slide over me. "Come on, Baby Girl. You're not finished yet."

I think I whimper, but I'm not sure. Yes, Mason and I have had a lot of amazing sex this last month or so, but nothing this powerful, this vulnerable, this explosive before.

But, I can't hide the ripple of lightning that shoots through my body, straight to my core. My pussy to clenches around nothing as warm hands smooth up my back, massage my shoulders for a minute, then wrap around my waist to lift me up.

Suddenly, I'm floating like a ragdoll. Which is kind of funny because I am no size 10, but Gage always had a way of making me feel beautiful and comfortable in my own skin. Heck, Mason did, too.

"Are you ready, Baby Girl, or do you need to recover?" He whispers in my ear.

"Please. I need more, Sir." I murmur, already needy and aching for more.

"Good Girl." He punctuates the words with a gentle kiss, then flips me over. I land in Mason's arms with a yelp, and it takes me a moment to find equilibrium.

But, once I do, *holy shit, I'm in heaven.*

Mason's strong legs bunch and flex underneath my tender ass. His cock juts up, resting against my back as he pulls me to lie back on his chest. His warm hands find my breasts, and he begins fondling them as he groans out, thrusting up with the movement.

Gage, on the other hand, is now stripped free of his boxers. His massive dick, lined with six barbells making up his Jacob's ladder, stands tall and firm and...tantalizing.

Damn, I missed that dick.

Mason groans as Gage chuckles, and I belatedly realize I must have said that out loud. But I'm not embarrassed. It really is a pretty dick. At least seven inches fully hard with all that glorious metal. It's enough to make any girl cream herself.

And I almost do.

Instead, Mason begins tweaking my nipples, bringing me out of my perusal as I lean my head back against his strong shoulder.

"Hi, Angel," He whispers in my ear.

"Hi, Baby," I groan in return, rotating my hips in his lap, trying and failing to get some friction on my pulsing clit.

"What's the matter, Baby Girl?" Gage teases like a big jerkface.

"P-please." Yes, there's a lot of begging with Gage in the room. Fucker just loves to hear me beg like a bitch in heat. Not that I'm complaining. I love it, too.

"I don't know. Maybe Mason isn't ready...Mase?" He trails off, leaving Mason to decide my fate.

I moan long and loud as Mason licks a path from the middle of my neck up to my ear. He sucks my lobe into his mouth and releases an almost whiney. "Please, Sir. I need her wet pussy clenching around my cock."

His filthy description causes my pussy to clench, and I groan low in my chest. I had no idea hearing them talk about me like I'm not here would be such a fucking turn-on.

"Thank you for asking. Now, Chloe I need you to wrap your feet around Mason's calves, let me see our pussy."

I'm halfway to another orgasm already. I'm literally soaking and am moments from combusting. So, I do what he says.

Anything, anything he says, I'll gladly do.

Once my feet are secured and my pussy is bared for this man, everything goes still.

In my floaty state, it takes me a moment to force my eyes open and see Gage staring at me.

No, not at me; into me. He's staring into my soul, and right now, I feel more vulnerable, more raw than I ever have in my life.

My body temperature increases, and I can feel the blush bleeding a trail from my cheeks, down my neck, and spreading across my chest.

After another breath, Gage swallows audibly, looks back and forth between Mason and me, and says, "Fucking perfect." Then, he immediately drops to his knees in front of us.

"Up," He commands, tapping on my inner thigh, and I work to raise my ass. As soon as it's up enough, he reaches between us and retrieves Mason's leaking cock! I feel the sticky pre-cum slide across my ass as Gage drage his cock to my entrance.

"Down." And then, I'm taking in Mason's fucking amazing dick deep inside my pussy. I whimper as the stretch stings me, and pain mixes with pleasure.

Mason groans, squeezing both of my breasts until it's almost painful but I don't dare safeword.

It's too much, but not enough.

Too vulnerable, but so damn right.

I feel another gush explode out of me just as Mason fills me completely. My pussy clenches around his shaft, and I swear I feel the barbells of his magic cross rubbing against my inner walls.

My hands shake, my legs quake and my pussy quivers as Mason and I wait for the next command. Our harsh pants mix with the silence of the room, and just when I'm about to lose my ever-loving mind, Gage leans in.

My focus is hazy at best, but what he does next causes an instantaneous reaction. I can't even question what he's doing because flashes of light spark behind my eyelids as he sticks his tongue and licks a path from somewhere below me, all the way up to my clit, then back again.

And my body sings!

Mason's throaty groan, mixed with the taboo nature of Gage tonguing both of us, sets off my second orgasm of the night.

It's a delicious mixture of beauty and weightlessness as my pussy repeatedly constricts around Mason's dick.

Gage doesn't even let up. Instead, he continues licking slow, leisurely paths up and down the area where Mason and I are joined, drawing out deep, guttural moans from Mason and prolonging my orgasm.

Eventually, Gage lifts away, looks up at both of us, and barks, "Move."

His gaze bores into Mason's, conveying some kind of silent communication. By his next blink, Mason fucking moves... oh, he fucking moves!

He wraps his arms around my waist, lifts me just a little, and begins pounding up into me. He's a jackrabbit as he fucks up into me, and I feel every barbell, every vein, every damn thrust.

I'm a panting, breathless mess, and it's all too much. But, not enough. I crave more. I need more!

Gage leans back in and doubles down on his efforts. Licking, sucking, slurping my clit and, what I assume is Mason's balls.

"So good. So good." I whimper out nonsensical sounds as my body is used for pleasure.

Just then, Mason takes one arm and brings it up, circling his hand across the front of my throat and squeezing the sides. My brain goes from floaty to pure euphoria as I close my eyes and let these men completely take over my pleasure.

Time ceases to exist as Mason continues to use my body and Gage continues to abuse my clit.

And then, fireworks...

Fireworks burn brighter than ever behind my eyes as another orgasm completely consumes me.

29

~Mason~

Chloe's orgasm sets off a chain reaction. Her pussy clamps down on my cock, milking me for all its worth. I should feel embarrassed that I came so quickly but, to be honest, I'm not.

Pleasure like nothing I've ever felt tingles down my spine and bursts from my balls with each wave of Chloe's orgasm.

A few breaths later, I'm blinking out of my daze as a cold, wet cloth causes me to jump with a hiss through my teeth.

My eyes fly open and I peer around Chloe's half-asleep form to find Gage grinning to himself as he cleans us up.

He must feel my eyes on his as he gazes up at me through his lashes and I gasp at the raw, open emotions he's showing me.

"Up," He whispers, tapping my leg.

I gently wrap both arms around a sweaty, delectable Chloe, and we both groan out as my dick slides out of her warmth.

Over the next couple of minutes, Gage sweetly cleans us both up, then lifts Chloe from my lap; walking her down the hall, and tucking her in our bed.

My eyes close, and I take a deep, rejuvenating breath through my nose as I wait for him to return.

"You did good, Baby Boy," He murmurs in my ear, causing my smile to grow wide.

"Thank you, Love." Sighing against his warm, calloused hand against my face, I say, "I love you."

Gage leans down, meeting my lips in a gentle kiss, and whispers back, "I love you, too."

Opening my eyes, I meet his gaze and smirk. My eyes flick down to his still-hard, angry-looking cock; then I make my move.

"Allow me, Sir." I purr as I slip from my armchair, bracing my hands behind his thighs and taking him all the way into my wet, waiting mouth.

The metallic taste of his Jacob's ladder makes my body zing as my cock springs back to life. I make sure I lavish each individual piercing with my tongue before sucking him hard, maneuvering back until the tip pops out of my mouth.

His groan rumbles through his body and I smile at knowing I definitely still affect him. *We both do.*

Tonguing the tip, I lick off a drop of pre-cum and play with his slit until he hisses out, running his hands into my hair and pulling me forward.

I chuckle as I take him back into my mouth, hollowing out my cheeks and allowing the tip to hit the back of my throat once, twice, three times until I'm gagging. He pulls my hair to help me off, and his eyes zero in on the string of spit running from my mouth to his beautiful cock.

I watch, mesmerized, as his jaw clenches, his eyes darken, and his forearm veins jump from restraint. Then, he slams his cock back into my waiting mouth.

And fuck me do I love it.

Gage uses my mouth like it's his own personal fleshlight.

"That's my Good Boy. Fuck! This mouth is sin." He grunts between thrusts.

"That's it. Take my cock. I own this mouth as much as I own that ass. Isn't that right?" His ramblings are punctuated by harsh pants, and the bunch in his thighs tell me that he's very, very close to losing it.

"Mmmm," I hum around his length, allowing him to forcefully thrust in and out of my mouth.

And, just like that, his balls draw up, tapping against my chin, and his hot, sticky semen floods my mouth.

I wait like he's taught me to, with my mouth filled with his cum, until he releases his dick from my mouth. Opening wide, I show him his own load, and he leans down in front of me. "Swallow," He rasps.

And I do. The salty, sticky substance slides down my throat, and I feel higher than any kite I've ever flown, and I'm more than happy to stay right here, in this moment with him.

With another kiss, Gage stands above me and smiles his signature loving smile. The one almost no one has the pleasure of witnessing.

He offers me his hand in a silent gesture as he looks at me like I'm his everything. And, in this moment, I feel like I am.

As soon as I'm standing, we stroll to the guest bathroom, hand-in-hand. After we enter, Gage runs me a phenomenal Epsom salt bath; never breaking our connection. He always knows just the perfect temperature to set it that has me completely melting and healing in all the best ways.

As the bath fills, he turns toward me, takes two steps, then slams his lips to mine.

"Let's get you cleaned up then in bed, ok?" He rasps after breaking the kiss. Turning away, he shuts off the water, winks, and offers his hand to help me get into the bath. We both slide into the oversized tub, facing each other, and lean back with contented sighs.

His hands find my feet and begin massaging each one as I relax even more into the rejuvenating bath.

My head lolls back with a thump, and I let myself get lost in his touch as we both recover from the scene.

My eyes flutter open at the sound of Gage's quiet voice on the phone. Opening my eyes just a little more, I see him leaning over his knees, sitting on the opposite side of the bed.

It takes a moment to realize that I'm wrapped around Chloe, spooning her from behind.

Her fantastic ass is up against my dick, and she is still beautifully naked. Gage and I only put on our briefs before climbing in for a post-scene nap.

"Yes, Don." I hear him murmur.

A second later, he sets the phone on the nightstand. Gage sighs deeply, like he's exhausted, and rubs a hand through his hair. I watch as he maneuvers his head back and forth, whispering under his breath, before standing and making his way to the closet.

Knowing what a conversation with the Don means, I take a deep, relaxing inhale; Chloe's sensual lavender scent blanketing me.

Extracting myself from her warm, perfect body is one of the most difficult things I've ever had to do.

Meeting Gage in the closet, I find him already in a pair of dark gray slacks and a crisp, white button-up. Just as he removes a matching gray suit jacket from its hanger, he spins around to face me.

With a wide smile, I step into his space and kiss him until we're both breathless.

When we break apart, I look deep into his eyes and see that worry written all over his face.

"Meeting?" I whisper into the dimly lit closet.

He sighs, nods his head, and looks down at his feet. "Yeah. *All* of us."

It takes my brain a moment to snap into action as I realize the gravity of that statement. *Don wants us to bring Chloe in.*

I have always trusted Don and known him to be an honest man, but that doesn't stop the anxiety from swirling in my gut about taking Chloe to him.

Not when she still has an active hit out on her.

I strain my neck, peer out into the room, and take in Chloe as if it's the last time.

Her angelic face is peaceful as she sleeps. The splotches of red no longer cover her creamy skin, and her face is framed with locks of messy hair.

My eyes travel over her delectable curves, her perfect breasts with those deliciously dark pink areolas, and the way her belly ring glints in the light.

She is stunningly perfect.

And, at this moment, I'm not sure I wouldn't turn on Don if it meant protecting her.

30

~Chloe~

Thirty minutes ago, I woke up to the best smell ever: fresh coffee with a splash of Vanilla creamer. Admittedly, I was not impressed by being woken up from my post-sex scene slumber but, the coffee at least saved Mason from getting his dick chopped off.

Of course, when Gage slowly slid onto the bed, held my hand, and looked at me like I was a rare jewel, I swooned and then preened at the sweet, gentle kiss he placed on my lips.

Then he dropped yet another bomb on me.

His Don wants to meet me. As in, he leader of the Italian Mafia!

Now, here I am, at some "non-descript location" with a blindfold over my head, being led to my certain death.

Or so my over-active imagination believes.

Regardless, Gage and Mason are both squeezing each of my hands as we stand in the elevator.

Ding

Ding

Ding

Ding

The elevator continues to climb, much like my heart rate. Thankfully, the guys' scents, sandalwood, leather, mint, and something so inherently male, seem to help ground me.

We pass another floor in silence, as discussed, and finally appear to be coming to a stop.

I've lost count of how many floors we actually went up, but judging from the dinging still vibrating through my ears, this is one very tall building.

The elevator lurches to a stop, and I squeeze the guys' hands even harder as nerves riot through my belly.

"It's ok, Baby Girl. We'll be here with you the whole time." Gage whispers in my ear, then places a gentle kiss on my temple.

"Yeah, Angel. No worries. We've got you." Mason whispers in my other ear. He leans in, his warmth radiating off of his skin, and gives me an equally sweet kiss on my other temple.

My ovaries just had a party, and this is not the time to think about these two mirroring each other in a scene. *Yummm.*

Mason chuckles under his breath, his warm breath tickling my neck as he murmurs, "I can see what you're feeling all over your pretty neck. Don't you worry, Angel, we'll take care of our dirty girl as soon as we get home." He chuckles again just as the doors whirr open.

The air thickens with tension, and something smoky hits my nostrils. Something like cigars and expensive cologne.

We walk about twenty steps before I hear Gage shift on my right. A knock rings out in the otherwise silent space, and I'm momentarily proud of myself for not flinching at the sudden sound.

"Enter," a faceless, muffled voice calls out through what I can only imagine is a thick door.

The air shifts around us as the door swings open, and we're ushered into another room.

The door closing loudly behind me does cause me to flinch this time, but both of my men squeeze my hands again... right before they drop them and appear to step away.

"Don," Gage says firmly.

"Don," Mason repeats.

And then, I'm blanketed in an eerie silence.

After about two minutes of nothing but the beating of my own heart to keep me company, someone breaks the tension.

I feel Mason's warmth next to me for a second before his gentle hands begin working to free me from the blindfold.

Blinking rapidly, I fight against the blinding light.

Eventually, my vision focuses on a bright room with floor-to-ceiling windows that overlook a part of town I am definitely not familiar with.

In the middle of the room sits a large oak desk that screams antique, and two men flank the sides with their arms crossed in front of them. Both men wear jet-black suits, white shirts, and the shiniest shoes I've ever seen.

One man looks like he's gone five rounds with a pulverizer; the whole left side of his face burned and scarred. His hair is cut military short, and his face and eyes appear to be completely blank.

The man on the right also has a short haircut with empty eyes but is sporting a gnarly scar running from his hairline all the way through his right brow. It's jagged and pure white, like it's been there for a while.

Finally, my gaze tracks to the man behind the desk. He's sitting down, but I'd bet my life savings that his suit costs more than my car. It screams money, danger... and power.

The lights cause the fat, golden ring on the man's pinky to glimmer; shining out through the darkness.

His suit is also jet black and probably matches the color of what his hair used to be. Now, it's salt and pepper colored with a few streaks of black combed through. This man has a beard that is shaved close to his face, which is also magnificently salt and peppered, giving away his older age.

When I feel I'm brave enough, I lock gazes with the man who also appears to be appraising me somehow. His emerald green eyes appear to be kind, but there's a severe darkness to them that makes me shiver.

Mason and Gage haven't moved a muscle or said anything else since we first arrived, so I take my cue from them.

Don's gaze appears to assess every bump, freckle, and wrinkle of my body and clothing, and I'm suddenly thankful that the guys had a surprise wardrobe hidden just for me.

I'm a bigger woman, I know this, but this red dress is perfect for hiding all the flab and showing off just enough of my assets that it's both sexy yet professional.

And the flare: Well, yes, I did twirl in the mirror before the reality of my situation had sunk in.

The seconds seem to tick by in my brain as we all wait for Don to do or say something. My skin is starting to flush with his perusal, and my cheeks flame with embarrassment and uncertainty.

Just when I fear I may pass out, he flashes a brilliant smile and claps his hands, effectively making me jump. Then he shouts, "Principessa! Welcome home!"

Brain Offline

"Um, uh, what?" I stammer out.

Yes, I know the guys said I was some traitor's daughter, but...this guy seemed to say *Principessa* like it was personal.

He laughs out loud, his green eyes sparkling with joy as he pushes to a stand, unbuttons his suit jacket, and rounds the desk.

"I promised your Mama I would wait until you were 25 to make contact. And then, you disappeared for a while." His tone drops to a menacing growl as he narrows his eyes at Gage.

"Excuse me?" I squeal. Either this man is fucking with us all, or, or...

I look over at Gage to see his face pale, and his brows raise just a hitch.

"Did you know?" I whisper-yell for some reason.

He glances sideways at me, keeping perfectly erect and giving nothing away. He doesn't keep eye contact as his eyes flee mine and land back on the Don.

"Of course not! No one did. Now, come, come. I want to hear everything!"

He quickly ushers me into another room, and, based on the footsteps behind me, all four men follow.

With a flourish, he opens a huge wooden door and guides me through a spectacular living room. It's the exact opposite of the office, other than the floor-to-ceiling windows.

It's so large I swear you could fit a hundred people in here. And the light coming in from the wall-o-windows is stunning.

The walls are a rich, creamy color with golden framed paintings adorning them.

There's a massive Maroon leather couch on one side of a ginormous, rectangular rug. A curved, glass table with golden legs sits just in front of the couch, with four equally beautiful maroon leather chairs on the opposite side.

I vaguely process that there's a bar cart in the far corner and even a fireplace on the wall opposite the door we came through.

Don ushers me over to sit on the left side of the couch. Then, he removes his suit jacket and tosses it to one of the stoney-faced men, who catches it without blinking.

Sitting down with a cushion of space between us, he leans forward and smiles wide. "My, my. You really took after your mother."

My brain registers the words, and his soft voice, and his kind eyes, but... it's just not computing.

"Oh, dear. Um, I'm messing this up. Ok, Sal, I need a drink for me and a Tequila Sunrise for my daughter."

That word: *Daughter.* That's the one that snaps me out of my stupor.

"What the fuck, Gage?" I stand outraged and stomp over to one of the two men I've given my heart to.

Angry tears burn in my eyes, but I push them back.

Once I'm toe-to-toe with him, I spit out, "You lied to me! You said I was a rat's kid. What the fuck?! Did you know? Is that why you slept with me?"

His eyes shine with unshed tears as mine begin to fall.

But he doesn't utter a word. He just stares straight ahead; at Don.

"Answer me!" I yell.

I hear a shuffling sound behind me but pay it no mind. I'm staring deeply into Gage's eyes as Don's hand finds my shoulders, and he slowly turns me to face him.

"No, Princepessa. They didn't know. No one did except for Sal and Al." Don states gently, boring into my soul with his eyes as his hand moves between his two minions.

Turning, I set my gaze on Gage, then Mason, before returning back to Gage. "But, I thought..."

I trail off as a lone tear tracks down Gage's face, causing my lip to tremble.

"Gage, Mason, I know there's a lot to discuss, but for now, can I have some time with my daughter?"

At first, neither of them move. They barely blink as they stand there like soldiers waiting for battle.

"Ora!" Don shouts, causing me to jump.

"Yes, Don," They say in unison. Then, they quickly turn on their heels and slip out of the large room and back into the office with Sal and Al.

"Come, come. We have much to discuss. And don't be so hard on the guys. They're ordered not to breathe, let alone talk, without my say-so. They are good soldiers. Soon to be good, Capos. But that's a story for another time. Come, sit. Sit."

I blearily walk back to the couch, flopping on it before noticing a perfect-looking drink made just for me, sitting on a little coaster on the table. With shaky hands, I take a sip, then another, and another.

Finally, I put it back on the coaster and face...*my Father?*

31

~Gage~

My girl. *My girl's the actual Princess! How the hell...*

"Did you know?" Mason barks while pacing. He's pulling at the roots of his hair, and I know he's spinning out.

Hell, I'm spinning out.

"No," Is all I can mutter. Part of me wants to calm him, but the storm raging in my mind and my heart is all I can hear.

He said she was a traitor's daughter. What the actual fuck? I mean, I know I don't have clearance, but... I've been with her for years. I've been tracking her since she turned 20 and have been with her since her 21st birthday. How the hell did I miss this?

Mason abruptly stops in front of me, grabs me by my face, and touches our foreheads. His eyes search mine, and I can see the turmoil raging in them. "Please, please tell me you didn't know," he whispers.

Lifting my hands to place them on his, I assure him, "I didn't. I swear it." Then, I move my lips over his, keeping the kiss soft, chaste, and full of conviction. As soon as I remember where we are, I pull away and give him a small smile for reassurance.

Suddenly, loud thumping comes from the room we just left moments ago.

Then, the door swings open with a loud *whoosh*.

"Get in here." Don grits his anger through his teeth, and I mentally prepare to be killed.

"Uh-uh. Don't even start that shit. You sent Gage to me. He said you knew we were dating!" Her screams echo around the penthouse, and I know Mason's eyes are as wide as mine.

Mason and I quickly shuffle into the next room to see an irate, almost petulant-looking Chloe.

Once the door closes, she marches straight over to the Don, lifts her finger, and pokes him in the chest. "You don't get a say in my life. I know, I know, you had to do it to keep Mama and me safe, but Gage has always been there. And Mason, well, that's new but my feelings for him are just as strong." I feel myself perk up a little at the fire my girl has.

My eyes briefly glance over to Mason, whose brows are now basically hidden by his hairline, as his chest puffs up a little with pride.

Leaving Don in a huff, she whips around, takes the two steps over to me, and pulls me in for a hard, bruising kiss. I'm stunned and stupid, and my brain can't process how to reciprocate before she pulls away, stomps over to Mason, and gives him the same treatment.

To say our girl's balls are big may be an understatement, but whatever; if she's really his daughter, he'll have to learn to accept her the way she is.

Fiery temper and all.

Like the badass I always knew she was, she walks back to the couch, sits down, crosses her legs, and gulps the rest of her drink down. The *clink* of the glass against the coaster damn near fractures my resolve to stand quietly like we're taught.

After a very tense silence, Don sighs from behind me, pats Mason and me on the shoulder, and presents his hand toward the chairs, a quiet command to sit.

"I'm sorry, Principessa. I'm still a Father. I have always kept tabs on you ever since we put your mother in the system. We had a huge war going on, and not all families believe that women and children should be spared." With a loud sigh, he rubs his head and moves back toward the couch.

She tracks his movements with her eyes, her anger dimming with each step.

Once he sits back in his position, he continues. "So, we hid you from the world; I needed to know that you were safe. Five years ago, someone hacked into the medical records of every hospital in the state. I guess they did a whole lot of fuckin' digging because the bastards were able to tell who your mother was. Once I saw her info on the dark web, I knew I had to get closer. I had to put more men in places but didn't want anyone turning rat on me. So, I made the decision to say you were the daughter of a rat. That way, no one would ask questions."

Lifting his tumbler off the table, he downs his scotch. Rolling the glass between his hands, he hangs his head. I swear I hear a sniffle just before he murmurs, "When they killed your mother, I lost it. I became a whole ass animal. I couldn't let that happen to you. Gage here," He says while tipping his head toward me, "Was around your age and truly one of the best men I've ever had working for me. He rose through my ranks, and I trusted him with you whole-heartedly. So," he inhales deeply, closes his eyes like he's in physical pain, and continues. "So, I had him befriend you. I fed him the same garbage as all the other men, but I told him I needed him closer to you in case you had heard from your father. I needed to make sure he wouldn't just watch but be involved."

Shaking his head, he rubs the back of his neck and rolls his head from back to front. "When he first said he was interested, I kind of wanted to shoot him. Then, I remembered how I felt about him. There was a reason I trusted him with you. And, honestly, there's no one else I'd wish my girl to be with."

"And, Mason?" She hedges quietly.

I see Mason's back go rigid, mirroring mine. Apparently, she told him we were all a thing. *Fuck.*

He takes a long, slow breath and releases it loudly, then hangs his head again and rests his elbows on his knees.

"Same with him. Is that what I envisioned for me, girl? No. But, if they make you happy, and they better..." He trails off with a glare that would have lesser men pissing themselves. "Then, I'm happy for you. But, if they step one foot outta line..." He starts with a finger jutting at me.

She quickly sits up, covers his hand with hers, then intertwines them. "They won't."

He looks shocked as he stares down at their joined hands then slowly up at her. With a smile I've seen more today than I have in the last three years, he nods and murmurs, "OK."

3²

~Chloe~

We spent another hour with my, um, Dad. He brought his on-call doctor in to do some blood tests to prove paternity but, Dad was completely confident of the results.

And maybe I'm being naive, but I believe him. I really do.

Of course, seeing pictures of him with my mother around the age she was when I was conceived didn't hurt. Neither did the marriage certificate with the name I know she went by before I was born.

Sitting on my bed, I absent-mindedly pick at a thread on my blanket as I think about how much my life has changed in less than a month.

New love interest.

Re-kindled an old love interest.

Was kidnapped by said love interests.

Finding out they're part of the Mafia.

Meeting my father.

Learning he sits on the throne of the Mafia.

Then, oh, and then, finding out I was the heir to said Mafia throne.

I mean, three years ago, I ran away when Gage shot someone. Can I handle being the boss? Can I handle *any* of this?

A soft knock on the door pulls me from my swirling thoughts. "C-come in." I stutter out somehow.

"Hey, Angel." Mason's soft voice filters through the room and immediately calms my storming thoughts.

"Hey, Baby," I murmur with a small smile.

"You ok?" He questions as he slides onto the bed.

I take in a restorative breath, blow it out, and allow my lungs to completely deplete before breathing again. "I think so. I..."

I stop, chewing on my lip as I try to gather my thoughts.

"I don't think I'm a wallflower, but I don't think I'm a good fit for the Mafia. Let alone the head of the Mafia. Did you hear him, Mase? He wants to train me to *be* him. To takeover! Is he nuts? Shouldn't he pass that down to someone who could actually do this? Who has been doing this? I mean, what the hell do *I* bring to the table?"

I flop back onto the bed with a *thump* and stare at the ceiling.

After a moment, Mason quietly joins me, lying beside me so our arms are touching.

Silence fills the space around us as my thoughts go from chaotic to quiet, then back again.

I hear Mason take in a deep inhale before saying, "I don't know what you're feeling; I've never been in your shoes. I know I haven't known you long... But I do know you're brave. I know you're strong. And I know that you are absolutely someone that I'd willingly stand beside and behind. You left that night Gage shot the guy. You didn't cry, you didn't scream, you didn't call the cops. You ran to safety. And, damn, that makes you strong as fuck in my book."

I have nothing to say to that, so I don't. Instead, I turn over and snuggle into Mason, allowing him to wrap his arm around me while I rest my head on his shoulder.

33

~Chloe~

Blinking my eyes open, I find myself aloneiin my room, tucked in underneath the covers. I blow out a deep breath, then fling off the covers and sit up, rubbing the sleep from my eyes.

There's a phone and a note with my name on it on the nightstand.

Over the last two months, Gage and Mason have made all kinds of little changes to the house and to my room.

Ok, that still sounds a little weird.

Where the room, and even the house, was contemporary yet void of any personal touches, there are now multiple pieces of furniture in my room and pictures of us decorating the walls. We haven't been able to get out much, other than to meet my father, so most of the pictures have been taken right here in this house, where we've yelled, laughed..., and loved.

It's been a lot for all of us, considering we're on a house arrest of sorts. We can still leave occasionally, but if we go somewhere public, Dad or his men have to be able to either defend it or be there within a moment's notice.

The good news is, although each week brings more hitmen, the ones who are captured bring us a little closer to the Russian asshole who has a hit out on me.

I feel my smile grow across my face as I think about how thoughtful and wonderful they have been. How accommodating and loving...

Maybe I won't move out after the Russians are taken care of. Unless, of course, they ask me to.

Leaning over, I grab the note. It must be from Mason because I would recognize Gage's writing:

My Angel,

Didn't want to wake you. We have a meeting to go to.
Gage wants you to meet us at 10 at STL.
You're already down as his guest
Dress in something sexy.

—M

My smile is full-on dopey at this point, but, dammit, they are too much.

And I can't lie, I'm excited about going to Sky's the Limit again. It's been far too long since I've had fun; since we've been able to go out.

Setting the note down, I pick up the sleek new phone. It's all black with a pocket of glitter on the back that moves around when pressed or tilted.

I chuckle and press the side button, seeing a picture of Mason and Gage making the most ridiculous faces I've ever seen, and I laugh out. Mason has his mouth pulled wide by his fingers, and Gage crosses his eyes and sticks his tongue out.

I check the contacts and see that I still only have three: Gage, Mason, and Don. At least when they gifted me the phone, they understood I wasn't ready to call him anything else.

Remembering his note, I let out a little school-girl giggle. I quickly jump up and bound out of the room. I hurriedly walk over to their room, which now holds a ridiculous amount of clothes that Gage and Mason bought for me. I have about two hours until I have to be at Sky's the Limit, our favorite club. But, wait....

Pulling my phone back out, I quickly text Gage.

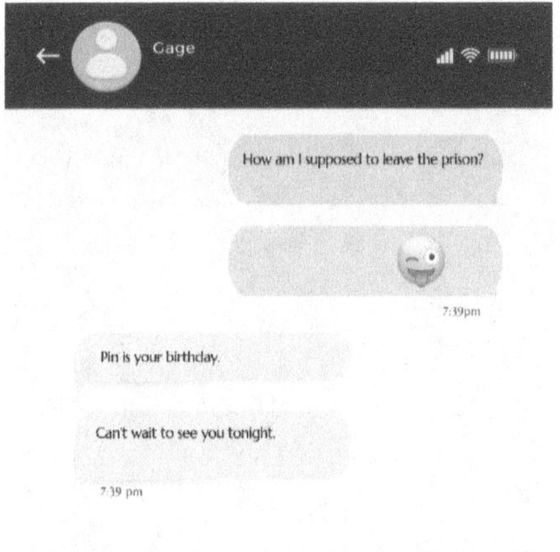

His response causes my heart to skip a beat, and I take a moment, biting my lip as I consider how impossibly sweet this man is. And how damn lucky I am.

Shaking myself away from the butterflies and girly stupor, I turn toward the clothes hanging in the closet and begin to piece together my outfit for tonight.

34

~Mason~

Don is still less than pleased that we were both in a relationship with Chloe. *I am still less than pleased that no one knew who she really was.* I get it, I really do, but damn, talk about being in the doghouse.

While Chloe slept off her very long, very revealing day, Don had us come in to talk strategy and "chat" with a man lurking around her old place.

Thankfully, one of the Capos had still been monitoring her old apartment and picked the guy up before he found out just how close she is.

After some persuasion from me, he finally gave us the name of his employer and how much he was getting paid. We were all less than pleased to find out that the price on Chloe's head is now at a cool million dollars. *Someone really wants to take Don down a notch.*

Since then, we've been working night and day on leads, hoping just one will point us in the right direction. We left the cameras up around her old apartment and job, and thankfully, that has proven to be more than fruitful. But, it's been oddly quiet for the last week, and we're all on edge.

It took some convincing but Gage finally talked Don into letting us take Chloe out. Of course, there is a promise to be on standby, but we also had to arrange for a few, let's say accommodations, for our stay tonight.

Now, we're headed to Sky's the Limit, our favorite club. We've never brought women back to the house when we decided to play, and now I'm glad. That's Chloe's space, and, in some ways, for Gage, it probably always has been.

Not that I can blame him now that I'm spending more time with her. She's brilliant, funny, flirty, shy, curious...everything.

She is everything.

Damn, I've got it bad.

Clearing my throat, Don's driver pulls into the lot and parks near the entrance. "Thanks, Reg, we'll have Tony drive us home." Gage throws out behind him as he clambers out of the car.

I chuckle to myself, shaking my head at his ridiculous nature but also understanding it completely.

Sliding out of the blacked-out car, I follow him to the door in the nondescript parking lot. It's packed here tonight, and for some reason, it only heightens my excitement.

Walking through the black, curtain-covered door, we're immediately face-to-face with Charlie. "What's up, man." He greets us with a firm handshake.

"Not much. Just needing to blow off some steam," Gage replies while looking almost antsy. He's always so stoic and ice-like when we aren't home, but I see that Chloe is slowly unraveling every fiber of what makes Gage an impenetrable force.

Charlie smiles wide and excitedly points out, "Chloe's here already. We sure have missed her around here."

I immediately perk up at her name, and Gage scowls slightly. "Where is she?" He's trying to sound calm and collected, but I can hear him grinding his teeth from here.

Charlie just chuckles, pats him on the back, and tosses his head behind him. "Last I saw, she was at the bar with Alma."

Gage visibly relaxes, causing me to chuckle, too. Then, he stomps over to our assigned locker for the night, tosses in his phone and keys, and waits for me to do the same.

Once we're finished, he locks it up, and I stop by him. "You ready, Love?" I coo in his ear, nibbling slightly. I take great satisfaction in watching his shoulders relax further as he lets out a small groan.

"You bet your ass I am."

We pick our band colors, deciding to go with black since we're both claimed- whether she knows it or not. Then, we walk through the thick, weighted curtain that was muffling some of the heavy bass.

Buy U a Drink by T-Pain bumps through the club, and at least a hundred bodies gyrate on the floor.

The now familiar red paint looks bloodier and more dangerous tonight, but that may just be because we recently tortured a man for hours.

Shrugging it off, I search the vast club for our girl.

I see Alma at the bar to my immediate left and head over to ask her about Chloel. "Hey, Alma. How's it hanging?" I ask, leaning over the bar.

She giggles and bats her eyes flirtatiously as she leans over the bar, her neon pink sports bra giving me, and every other person here, a healthy look at her cleavage.

We played once but never again. It was too messy since she works here. But we've stayed amicable friends since.

"Hey Maverick," she purrs, my club name rolling off her tongue all too suggestively. "It's good, but it could be better." She leans over, takes a cherry from the server, and pops it in her mouth.

I already know where this is going and see other members staring at her with desire. But I'm here for a different reason.

"So, I heard my girl was just over here. Know where she may have wandered off to?" I ask with a tip of my head to the dance floor.

Just as she reveals a perfectly knotted stem, someone clears their throat behind me. "Am I interrupting?" I smirk at Alma, knowing exactly whose voice that is.

Turning around, I lean against the bar, elbows resting on the counter as I take in the vixen standing in front of me.

She's in red heels that have a little strap running across each foot. Her skintight black jeans do nothing to hide her curves and her top shows the perfect amount of cleavage and her delectable collarbone. To top it all off, her beautiful, silky hair is flowing down to her shoulders in soft waves.

But the thing that really gets me is that she's wearing a black band, too.

I groan and bite on my knuckles. "Damn, Angel. Did you wear that for me?" I bite my lip to tamp down the raging hormones and try to tell my dick to calm the fuck down. It's nowhere near midnight, and judging by the fire in Chloe's eyes, I may be in trouble, too.

I hear Alma clinking glasses together, and then she appears at my side..."Oh!!! This is one of your guys, Lo?" She chirps, chuckling afterward. "He was just asking about you. And, before you get all she-man on me, we don't mesh like that. But that doesn't mean I don't love to give the patrons a good show." She crows just as a bunch of cheers go up around us.

Turning around, I see her stick a long neck between her breasts, tip it up, and drink it down in three long gulps.

Chuckling at her antics, I turn back to my girl, narrow my eyes, and swagger to her.

"Mine," I growl just as I smash our lips together.

She tries to fight it at first, but I don't let her. If she wants a battle of wills, she's damn well going to get one.

Just as she relaxes into the kiss, I break it, leaning my forehead against hers. Whispering loud enough that she can hear me over the music, I say, "Charlie told me you were with her. I was standing there all of twenty seconds before you walked up."

Her eyes flutter open, and I'm struck by how fucking beautiful this woman is. I watch as a mischievous smirk graces her mouth, and she responds, "I know. I just needed *her* and *everyone else* around here to know. She seemed nice enough, but.... I figured I'd make it clear."

"Aww, baby, were you pissin' on my leg?" I chuckle and kiss her temple.

She laughs along and eventually says, "Not my kink, but if you really want to, I would...for you." And damn if my heart didn't jump out and give itself right to her.

I gently shake my head and am immediately clapped on the back. When the hand gives me a firm squeeze, I turn my head to see Gage; laughter shining in his eyes. *Fucker sat back and watched the whole thing. Bastard.*

Moving aside, I let Gage swoop in and kiss the breath right out of Chloe. He dips her down, and I hear her giggle as her leg raises high in the air.

Finally righting her, Gage turns back to me, Chloe's hand firmly holding his, and says, "Got us a booth in the far corner." He nods his head toward the corner opposite where we're standing.

It's a great spot, really. You can see the only two entrances and exits (barring emergencies) and all of the patrons. *Always on his game that one.*

Once we get to our table, a waitress promptly drops drinks off, and Gage pays her. Chloe slides into the booth as we each take a spot on either side of her, moving in nice and tight.

"Now, boys, don't be naughty just yet. We have dancing to do and plenty of time to do it before the other side opens up.

She takes her Tequila Sunrise and downs it. I barely blink before she disappears under the table and pops back out the other end.

"Come on guys, show me whatcha got." She yells over the speaker just as Candy Shop by 50 Cent begins. Her hips begin to move in time with the music in the sexiest manner, and I swear to all things un-holy, I'm going to cum in my pants. *Fuck this woman.*

With a groan, and a little bit of a wobble, I follow Gage as he prowls toward her. But my view is better.

I get to see her eyes dilate with a mixture of lust and excitement.

And I also get to watch Gage's tight ass walking away from me.

Maybe I should sit and just watch...

Nah.

35

~Chloe~

It's almost midnight and I am so, ridiculously, keyed up. Dancing with Gage has always been an erotic experience. But dancing between *them*, their bodies pressing against mine, surrounding me like a sexy Chloe sandwich, is heady as fuck. And I want more...

So much more!

We've talked, we've danced, we've people-watched and now, well, now I want to be touched, no, I want to be played like a damn guitar.

"Alright ladies and gentlemen, the moment you've been waiting for..." The MC calls out. "Be safe in there tonight. The Sky's the Limit." He jokes with a laugh before adding, "For those who are keeping the party going in here, grab a drink and *Shake That Ass*." Salt Shaker by the Ying Yang Twins immediately starts up as bodies move in three separate masses; one to the dance floor, another to the bar, and a third...to the black curtain hiding the other door.

The one that leads to sin and salvation.

Gage and Mason both stand, wrapping their hands in mine and giving me the most devilish smirks.

What do these two have up their sleeves?

Gage takes the lead and winds us through the growing crowd.

When we enter the door, Sexy Can I by Ray J streams through the room and sets a whole different vibe from the ass shakin' next door.

My whole body tingles with awareness as my gaze immediately travels over to the six golden cages that house the entertainers for tonight.

The dim lights along the perimeter of the floor make the red-painted walls look even sexier and the spotlights raining down on the dancers makes them look ethereal.

The one furthest away draws me. She's heavier set, like me- rolls, dimples, breasts, and thick thighs on display- but, also like me on stage, she's lost in the music; she's free.

The bar in the corner near her gets thicker but, I pay it no mind. I just creep closer, wishing desperately that I could be the one rubbing my hands up and down my mostly naked body and losing myself to the freedom of the music.

The woman is wearing a black sports bra with a mesh cutout and a tiny ass black skirt with a buckle around her left thigh. Her long, black hair flows down to her ass as her body moves to the music.

From my spot on the floor beneath her, I watch entranced as her fingers enter her pussy. I feel someone brush up against my back at the same time and I startle with a yelp, turning and finding Mason there. His hands are up in a gesture of peace and a wide smile is spread across his stupidly perfect face.

"See something you like, Angel?" He asks with a tip of his chin toward the woman behind me.

Turning back to her, I watch her as she slides two fingers in and out of her channel, massaging her breast with her other hand.

"Y-yes." I breathe out as his body pushes up against mine, his hands finding my waist.

"Is it her, or what she's doing?" He whispers in my ear as his left hand makes its way to my breast, brushing the pad of his thumb across my nipple.

They already found out that my bra is barely a slip of lace so it takes him no time to work my nipple into a taut peek.

"Um, what she's doing. I- I miss dancing." I whimper as his other hand begins dancing its way from my hip to the button of my jeans.

"Is that what you want, Angel? To dance for everyone here?"

"Y-yes," I murmur.

He pops the button off my jeans and tweaks my nipple through my shirt.

"Do you want to dance here, Angel? Do you want to pleasure yourself in front of all these people?" His hand forces its way under my pants to find my aching center.

"Yes, Oh God, Yes," I mumble as my pussy tightens around nothing.

Just then, he swipes his fingers across my clit and I moan out to the room.

All around us, people are in various stages of undress but...there's someone missing.

"Wh-where's Gage?" I ask as I thrust my wanting pussy into his fingers.

"He has a room. He wanted me to come find you." His fingers continue their barely-there perusal, and my arousal pools in my lacey thong.

"O-Ok. Let's go." I say, not moving an inch.

After a few more strokes of my clit, my toes curl as a man comes up and begins to play with the woman's ass.

Suddenly, I'm being hoisted in the air, and thrown over Mason's back. "Mason! Stop you, Oaf. I'm too heavy for that."

At first, I don't think he hears me until a loud, hard *thwap* lands on my ass. My yelp morphs into a moan as he rubs away the sting with his large hand.

"Don't ever say that again." He commands as he marches us through the throng of vibrating bodies toward the room Gage is waiting in.

36

~Gage~

Change (In the House of Flies) by Deftones begins to play softly in the candlelit room as I finish setting up the last few things. I want tonight to be perfect; it needs to be perfect.

As I finish tying off the last rope, the door behind me opens. I turn to find Mason with Chloe hanging, laughing like a lunatic, over his shoulder.

I just can't help myself; I stroll over to him, swat her juicy behind, and then pull him in for a deep, soul-altering kiss.

"Ok, you two, I'm getting a little lightheaded back here." Chloe sasses, and I hear the tell-tale signs of her swatting Mason's ass.

We both chuckle as we break the kiss, and I step back just in time to see Mason whap Chloe on the same side I just did before he rubs the spot, causing her to moan out. My cock hardens almost painfully in my pants, and I'm already worried I'm going to mess this all up by blowing too soon.

He quickly slides her down the front of his body, thrusting against her as she meets his groin. Once she's on her feet, she's already a panting, breathy mess, and my cock weeps.

"Mase, present." My Dom mask slips perfectly into place, and I watch, enthralled by his movements, as each article of clothing is stripped away.

Having Mason and Chloe together is a dream I never thought would come to life, but here we are, in my favorite club, and I'm about to do unspeakable things to both of them.

What a great day it is to be alive.

Mason steps over to the red, padded St. Andrew's Cross, folds his hands over the top beams, and sticks his ass straight at me.

The room is all black—walls, bedspread, nightstands, cabinets, curtains—making the red items pop—the bondage board, the cross, and even the shackles that adorn the black, leather-tufted headboard.

The candles I have placed around the room are all dual-purpose-light and temperature play; both of which we will absolutely be exploring tonight.

Looking at a still fully dressed Chloe, I see that she has also dropped to her knees, ass on her heels, hands resting on her wide-set thighs, and head bowed.

"My Good Girl. Want to help me secure him?" I ask her as I move a lock of hair away from her face, relishing in the way it feels between my fingers.

"Yes, Sir." She whispers.

I hold my hand in front of her face, a silent command to take it, which she does. I then guide her over to the cross, where Mason is still bent over, his sexy little hole on full display.

"See something you like, Baby Girl?" I ask as my eyes track the path of her blush, splotching its way from her face, down her neck, and to her chest.

"Y-yes, Sir."

I humm out, filing that away for later, and proceed to unravel the chains connected to the cross.

"Get into position," I tell Mason, growling a little as my desire heightens.

He moves immediately. Standing to his full height, he turns and raises his arms, allowing me to wrap the leather cuffs around his wrists and while Chloe secures his ankles. I don't bind him any further tonight. Tonight's complicated binding will go to my beautiful, sassy, fierce girl.

Nice n Slow by Usher begins to play, and I let the rhythm set the pace for what I do next.

Tonight, she finds out exactly how strong she is *And how perfect she is for both of us.*

And I'm going to take it painstakingly slow.

I've spent the last fifteen minutes moving between edging while binding Chloe and teasing Mason. After each row of knots is completed around Chloe's beautiful body, I look up to find Mason firmly locked into subspace. His eyes are blown wide, his panting is shallow, and you'd almost believe that I was doing more than stroking him a couple of times between each section.

Looking up at him now, I see his pre-cum leaking to the floor, and his body is trembling with needy lust.

"What do you think, Mase? Do you think Chloe's bindings are just about done?" His cock jumps for attention, and I can't help the smirk that crawls across my face.

"Yes, sir. P-please. Please touch me." He begs beautifully.

"Well, if I touch you, how will that make her feel? Do you think she'll feel left out?"

For a moment, he looks genuinely torn. A chuckle vibrates my chest as she moans from her spot on the floor.

"OK. OK. Easy, you two. Don't you worry, your *master* will take good care of you both."

I growled the word "master" because that's really what I want to be. I've never had the conversation with either of them, but it fits. I am theirs as much as they are mine.

Owned. Completely. Forever.

"Please," Chloe cries, a tear flowing down her cheek.

Squatting down, I take in her bound form and smile like a doofus. "You really are the most beautiful woman I've ever laid eyes on."

Her eyes lift high to find mine above her, and she smiles, although it does look strained.

Maybe I took the gentle grazes across her sex, her clit, her nipples, too far while I bound her up like a little sex puppet.

Maybe not.

Standing to my full height, I walk over to Mason, circling the cross, and watch with delight as he clenches his ass cheeks together.

"Mason, Mason, Mason. What shall I do with you? You're both tied up, completely at my mercy. But look at you, my sweet boy, dripping your pre-cum all over the floor underneath you." I *tsk* through my teeth at my very fake predicament. "I suppose we should get you cleaned up, yeah?"

Mason sucks in a shuddering breath, his cock waving toward Chloe like a white flag.

"Deal," I whisper in his ear. Then, I press biting kisses along the column of his neck while gently gliding my hands over his waist, up his taut abdomen, and begin to tweak his nipples.

"You've been such a good boy," I groan, my left hand traveling back down his abdomen to find his harder-than-steel cock.

"I'm going to give you exactly what you need," I say a little louder. My gaze travels to Chloe, who's still bound helplessly on the floor. And I'm not surprised to find her eyes on us. Her lip trembles, and I can tell she's trying to move around to get the friction on her needy clit.

"Perfect," I comment, stroking Mason twice before releasing him. His groan vibrates through my chest, and I smirk.

But, I just walk away.

"P-Please, Sir. I'll do anything. Please!" He cries out, causing the chains to rustle as he pushes against them.

"Ah, ah, ah. I've got you. Don't worry."

I take my time shuffling behind Chloe and notice that she, too, has made a little mess on the floor.

"Are you wet for us, Chloe? Is your pussy weeping for us? Weeping for our touch?" I coo sardonically.

"A sob rips from her throat moments before I take the longest rope and give it a good tug, hauling her body, strapped to the bondage board, up off the floor.

She yelps in surprise, and I check Mason's face to see if there is any concern. But, I see none. I see a man who has gone full-ass feral as he tugs against his bindings, his mind having blanked completely and his body in full control.

"Now, now, Mason. You'll get your turn with our little vixen."

That seems to calm him a little so the bindings won't mark his perfect wrists as badly. But, still, he likes the bite of pain.

I tug the rope once, twice, three more times until my girl is at the perfect height.

"Well, would you like at that, Mase?"

Chloe's gloriously naked body is trussed up like a Thanksgiving turkey. The bondage board would only be long enough for her chest and belly; if she were lying flat. But she's not. Instead, her shoulders are pressed into the top of the board, and she folds down with her knees spread on either side of her. The board hits her about two inches below the knees for stability, but her shins and feet are hanging off the board, allowing me very easy access to her dripping pussy and peachy, round ass. Her head falls off the board if she hangs it down, but right now, I can see it lifted and lined up... right with Mason's jutting cock.

Her head shakes a little from holding it up, but I have the perfect view of her pussy clenching around nothing.

"What do you want, Baby Girl? Do you want Mason's cock in your mouth? Or do you want my cock in your soaking wet pussy?"

"Both," She whimpers out. "Both p-please." Her head starts shaking back and forth like she can't take it anymore.

But, she can, I know she can.

"Oh, Baby. Have I pushed you too far? Do you want to safeword and stop?" I coo sarcastically.

"No! Please, no! Please, sir. Fill me up." Her squeals of frustration are almost as comical as Mason's purple-tipped dick.

Deciding that's enough edging, I swipe my fingers through her wet folds, earning a guttural groan from her. With her mouth open wide, I bump the table and watch as Mason's cock slides perfectly into her. He hisses with the contact, and she goes from groaning to moaning around his girthy dick.

Mason tries to thrust his hips, but he can't go far. So, like that good Master I am, I help him out a bit.

I push one thick finger into her waiting cunt and make sure to push a little harder than I normally would. The force causes the bondage board to swing, which, in turn, causes him to go deeper into her mouth.

I listen for their sounds of pleasure as she starts to slurp and tries to bob on his dick.

Sliding out, I add a second finger and start opening her up for me. She's already dripping down my hand but I pay it no mind. Instead, I begin finger fucking her with fervor.

With each thrust of my fingers, her mouth envelops Mason even more.

For a long moment, I get lost in the movement, in the sounds, at the sight of his cock disappearing into her mouth. I revel in their collective soundtrack of throaty, garbled moans and painfully pleasure-filled groans that echo out with every thrust of my fingers.

It's so fucking hot that I have no choice but to stop everything. Just for a moment. Just to keep from blowing my own load.

When I do, I watch as his dick falls from her mouth, and they both whimper and whine in response. Her head hangs low beyond the board and his falls back between his shoulders as they both pant for breath.

"My, my. You're both being so good for your master. Now, it's my turn." I grunt out through my teeth.

Freeing myself from my socks and shoes, I quickly strip out of my shirt and pants and watch in rapt satisfaction as Mason's eyes trail over my now-naked body.

The Weeknd's The Party and The After Party starts to play, and I smile wide because I love these two so damn much.

"You ready, Baby Girl? Can you take me fucking this pussy while you fuck his cock with your mouth?"

"Mm-hmm," She moans as more pre-cum drops off of Mason's cock.

"Good Girl. " I line up my tip up with her entrance just before slamming all the fucking way into her. She fits me like a damn glove, and her scream of pleasure echoes around the dimly lit room.

Once I bottom out, I have to grit my teeth to prevent myself from blowing too soon. I grab her hips, digging my fingers in as I tell my cock to calm the fuck down.

See, that's the problem with edging. Edging them also edges you. It's a painfully amazing experience that I swear I will never get enough of.

Blowing out a deep breath, I slowly retreat from her body, my barbells catching on every surface of the inside of her pussy as she clamps down around me.

She moans long and low as I slide out, then hisses through her teeth when I slam back in.

On my third pass, I command, "Take him, now, Baby Girl. Show Mason what a good girl you can be."

And, fuck me, she does.

Her mouth opens right before I slam back into her, and I watch as she swallows Mason whole.

Then, I set the pace hard and fast. I fuck into her like I'm a damn animal. Her throaty moans mixed with Mason's groans are like an erotic soundtrack that I would gladly listen to on repeat.

"Just like that, Angel. Suck my cock down." Mason's words cause her cunt to clamp down on me, signaling that she's close. So, I fold on top of her, move my right hand from her waist to her hood underneath, and begin flicking the tip of my finger across her clit; just like she likes it.

"Cum, now, Baby Girl."

I barely pull out, then back in again before her orgasm rushes over her.

I grunt and groan as her pussy clenches around me repeatedly, then tries to push me out.

So I let it.

I slide my cock out of her wet heat while continuing to flick her clit like a mini-vibrator, and she goes, the fuck, off! Her body locks up tight, and her breaths push out her mouth around Mason's cock.

Gush after gush of cum squirt out all over the floor, and my dick.

"Good job, Baby Girl. Now, take all of Mason's cum and swallow it like a dirty girl." Her moan of acceptance is muffled as he unloads in her mouth, and I smile as I listen to her swallow him down greedily.

And I couldn't be prouder than I am right now.

Just as she releases him with a wet pop, I slam back into her and fuck her with a renewed fervor. It doesn't take long. Her wet pussy welcomes me as I destroy it.

Finally, my spine tingles and my balls draw up painfully before spurt after spurt of hot cum rushes out of my hard dick.

I have to catch myself from smashing on top of her as my arms give out. Once I get the shaky bastards under control again, I lift my head and kiss gentle patterns across her shoulders and down her back as we both pant for breath.

I hear her whimper as I slide out of her and watch in rapt fascination as our combined release dribbles down her folds toward her clit.

With two fingers, I scoop it all back up and shove it back inside. "Mine," I growl like a ravenous beast before giving her a gentle kiss right on her peachy ass.

As I try to catch my breath, I look over at the two of them, and my heart swells within my chest. "Mine," I whisper, more to myself, as I take in the two people I know without a doubt that I want to spend my life with.

And I'll destroy anyone who thinks otherwise.

Mine.

37

~Mason~

Never in my life have I participated in something so damn hot before. I'd be lying if I said I didn't want to do it again.

Just...not right now. I need like a whole ass week to sleep and recover from that scene. I mean, I know we still have plans for temperature play and maybe some other things, but I'm too worn out to do anything but "hang out".

But, I would like to be released from the cross because Chloe...she just looks so damn helpless with her head hanging down off the bondage board.

The ropes that Gage rigged to the pully line above us dot each corner of the board so they all raise and lower at the same time. However, I feel like Gage will probably just lift her from her current position and start her aftercare. He's shaking like he was the one that was edged for hours before being allowed to cum.

Subspace is starting to clear, and I'm feeling...well, I'm feeling a lot. I want to kiss Gage and tell him I love him, but I'm torn with wanting to do the same with Chloe.

She totally and completely gave herself to us in the most beautiful display of trust, and she needs to know that I'll never take her for granted.

"Love, please," I croak out, my throat dry and in desperate need of water.

He's looking between us like we're something amazing and precious, and I feel the tears well up in my eyes.

He blinks a few times before he seems to come back to himself and realizes I said something.

"Oh, yes, right. Sorry." He grumbles apologetically.

Rushing over, he squats down and starts with my ankle cuffs, carefully unbuckling them and then gently massaging his fingers over the little indents that were left behind.

Chloe's soft snores echo behind him, and we freeze. From his position on the floor, he's at the perfect height to see her face so he lifts it gently, cradling her face in his hands before leaning in and giving her a gentle kiss.

He carefully lowers her head back down and smiles up at me before mouthing, "Sleeping." I half chuckle, knowing damn well how she feels, and begin rotating my feet around to get the blood circulating while Gage rises up and starts on my wrists.

Like the good Dom he is, he massages each wrist after they are freed and inspects for any cuts in the skin.

"Later," I whisper to him and lean in for a kiss.

He tastes like sin and danger, and I just want to bathe in it. But we can't. First, we need to free our girl.

It only takes a few minutes before Gage and I successfully free Chloe from her bindings. He carries her over to the bed and lies her down before rushing to the attached bathroom. I snuggled into her warm body and allowed myself to just be in this moment with her, sleeping in my arms.

Gage rushes back with two warm, wet cloths and gently cleans us both up. Then, he climbs in behind me, nuzzling into my neck and gives me a gentle kiss behind my ear.

"I love you, Baby Boy." He whispers as he begins slowly massaging my arms and shoulders.

Then, I remembered something I definitely wanted to ask about.

"Did you mean it?" I feel the lump in my throat as I think about him saying it was an accident; a slip of the tongue.

But, he surprises me, "Yes. I am yours, and you are mine. I claimed you both a long time ago. I just never knew how to ask if that's what you wanted."

My heart doubles in size, and I swear I can feel it thumping hard against my rib cage.

"I love you, Gage," I whisper as sleep begins to take me.

Thankfully, I hear him respond.

"I love you, too, Mason."

And then, I drift off to a blissful sleep between the two people I love more than life itself.

38

~Chloe~

A loud *boom* rattles the walls and startles me out of my sleep. I rush upwards with a gasp and look around. I see that Mason is on my left, and Gage is on the other side of him; still spooning him.

My heart feels like it's going to race out of my chest, and I'm dripping with sweat.

Shit, must have been a nightmare.

I will my heart rate to slow so I can snuggle back up to Mason but, before I can do that, another *boom* rattles the room and the fire alarms go off.

Mason and Gage whip up out of bed faster than I can blink.

They both scramble to their clothes and start tossing mine to me before I'm even off the bed.

No one says a word; we just go into battle mode.

Except me. Fuck. What the hell am I doing? I'm not trained to do anything other than run.

Boom!

Rat- Tat- Tat- Ta

Mason and Gage pause to look at each other, a silent conversation passing through them before they both nod and jump into action. Flying to the bathroom, they both take out an obscene amount of guns

174

from various hidey holes in and around the sink. "What the hell?" I screech.

Gage stands to his full height, walks back to me, and bends down, clasping my chin with his fingers. "Can you shoot?"

He asks, his eyes bouncing between mine.

"Um, well, I don't know." I ramble with my hands flying through the air.

Mason walks over and hands me a small pistol, and Gage points the gun toward the door quickly as he raises his voice over the sound of gunfire.

"Never *point* a gun unless you intend to shoot. Don't put your finger on the *trigger* until you're ready to shoot. Don't *shoot* at us." He says in a commanding tone before stomping toward the door.

I look back at Mason, knowing damn well my eyes are blanketed in fear. "Don't worry, Angel. We've got you. But, we know the owners, so, yeah, we're allowed to have backup."

Just then, he flips open a latch next to the nightstand, and a small, foldable phone falls out.

"Press 1. Tell him we need backup." He says before kissing the shit out of me and following Gage out of the door.

The door slams shut before I even have time to process.

The sounds of screams and the pinging of gunfire waft through the walls and cover the sounds of Lana Del Rey's Video Games. I guess they left the music on, and it makes a chilling contrast to the battle raging outside.

I suddenly remember holding the phone and quickly press 1.

"What?" A stern voice barks.

"We-we, um, need backup. Sky's the Limit." I shakily relay the message, and it feels like it's someone else.

"Chloe? Is that you, Principessa?"

"Dad?" I questioned, realizing too late what I called him and also realizing how whiney I just sounded.

"You have to come. They're in trouble. Please hurry." I ramble out before another blast blows the door off the hinges.

I scream and fall to the floor, clambering for the gun that I dropped and squeezing under the bed.

As the smoke clears, I hear thick, I think Russian, accents talking. At least two male voices, and for some reason that pisses me off. I hear the word "Princessa" and immediately go rigid. Oh, hell no. I just found my guys, and my Dad, there's no way in hell I'm going down without a fight.

And my resolve hardens.

If the guys can fight, so can I.

So, I do something utterly stupid. I aim for the guy closest to me, stick the gun out just enough to aim higher, and shoot out both kneecaps. One of the shells burns me on its way down, but I surprisingly don't scream as the adrenaline masks the pain.

Instead, I quickly scramble sideways to the other side of the bed, knowing the second man would probably shoot the spot I was just hiding under.

And I was right.

Pop-Pop-Pop

The bed stuffing fills the air as I crouch low next to the bed I've now slid out from. .

The overwhelming sounds of Russian shouting, and my heart beating in my ears, causes me to shiver violently; worried that I'm about to die alone.

Until I hear Gage's firm voice in my head.

Remembering what he said, I latch onto three specific words: *Point, trigger, shoot.*

They aren't even in here for me to fuck the last part up, so I focus on the two idiots on the other side of the bed.

My father is the head of the Mafia. You are not a wallflower. You are a fucking wildflower. Gage and Mason believe in you, they're counting on you. Go!!!

Then I rise up and fire off four shots into the back of the man who's standing and another shot into the head of the man who's screaming what I can only assume are Russian curse words.

For a whole ass eternity, all I can hear is a high-pitched ringing in my ears. The hand that the gun is in shakes violently, but I keep my grip firm.

Carefully toeing over to the two men, I see that one has dropped his gun, and I kick it away toward the bathroom before leaning over him to see the other man with his eyes wide…

Dead.

Bile splashes in the back of my throat, but I push it down because, holy shit, I think I just killed two people.

Two warm hands touch my shoulders, and I shriek as I twirl, bringing the gun out in front of me. A pair of concerned hazel eyes meet mine, and my brain finally kicks back on. "M-Mason?" I whimper before I take in a shuddering breath.

"Yeah, Angel. They're all gone. You're safe. Now, give me the gun." He says calmly but firmly. It's almost like he's scared of me.

Shit, *I'm* scared of me.

"O-OK," I stutter out, handing the gun over to him.

Once he has it tucked in his pocket, he flings his arms around my back and curls me into his body.

Something wet hits my cheeks as he pets my hair and whispers into my ear, "That's my girl. You did so well. Fuck! Did you get two of them? Fuck, that's hot."

I can't even process the words, yet, but, somewhere deep inside of me, I feel proud, loved, and safe.

39

~Gage~

After making sure the staff and other members were all safeoor tucked away in ambulances, I went searching for my girl.

Don showed up just in time to clear the mess with the police. It's crazy, really, because he looked more worried than pissed like I thought he'd be.

Don and his men help me clear each room again before I head into the one I left her in. The door has been blown open, and my heart falls out of my ass as awful visions of what I may see flash through my mind.

Don shoves me aside, screaming, "Chloe! Principessa, where are you?"

My stomach starts to revolt, but I force it down. I can't look weak in front of the Don or his men.

Finally, I hear, "Oh, my brave girl..." Followed by hushed voices.

Knowing that she must be alive, I force my feet to move and see two Russians on the floor with a hell of a lot of bullets in them.

Damn, that's my girl.

Then, I make my way to the bathroom where I hear the soft murmurs coming from, and step in to see Mason with a first aid kit laid out on the bathroom counter and Don embracing Chloe. "Thanks for coming, D-Dad." She hiccups between tears.

"Anytime, Prinicpessa. Every time."

And they stay wrapped in their embrace while Mason and I head out with the other men to give them space, and to start clean-up.

After Mason and I left the bathroom, we quietly closed the door, then began Russian Asshole Cleanup.

Lucky for us, my girl wasn't a perfect shot, so we had at least one critically injured; but not dead...yet.

He's now sitting in our basement, answering questions for Mason. And, when he doesn't want to answer, well, let's just say Mason is very good at making people talk.

It took twenty minutes to get all the Russian bastards out, then to tell Don we needed to move. He insisted that Chloe and him spend some time together so he could answer any questions she may have. I was reluctant, to say the least, since she hadn't even had proper after-care after our scene.

But, yeah, there's no way in hell I was telling Don that.

It's been two hours since we left them in that bathroom. I left Mason in the basement an hour ago while he continued torturing the only currently living Russian asshole. I just couldn't take my mind off of Chloe. She barely had time to process anything before being thrown in the middle of a Mafia war!

Now, I'm pacing the hallway, to the living room, to the kitchen... my mind running wild with everything and praying I'm wrong.

Is she ok? Will she run again?

Fuck! I'm losing my mind.

I hear the whirr of the electronic locks on the front door and run over to meet Mason.

Only, it's not Mason who greets me. A sexy, badass woman stands before, looking tired but wearing a sassy smirk.

"Honey, I'm home," she states quietly. Her eyes hold love, acceptance, and clarity and I can't help but march over to her, wrap my arms around her, and steal a bruising kiss.

She moans into my mouth, and I take over, plunging my tongue into hers as we fight for dominance.

But, as usual, I win.

When it becomes too much, I break the kiss. We both pant for air, her cheeks a ruddy red color, as we stare into each other's eyes.

"I-I love you, Chloe. I have since the first day I met you. And I never stopped. I never will stop."

I'm not sure why I'm laying my heart out right now. I think, maybe, I'm afraid she'll leave again.

"I love you, too, Gage. Always have, always will. Forever." She says before slamming her lips back to mine.

My phone rings, and I groan, grumbling at having to break the kiss but knowing it may be the Don.

Instead, I see it's Mason.

"Hey, Baby. Chloe's home." I say cheerfully into the speakerphone.

"Chloe! I missed you!" He cheers. It sounds like he's dancing around the basement, which causes me to chuckle and roll my eyes.

"It's been like two hours, Goober." She chides good-naturedly.

"I know but, still. Are you, um, are you ok?" He asks, almost unsure of himself. I can picture him chuffing his shoe across the ground like a little kid talking to a crush.

"I am." She responds with a whole-ass smile. "But, when are you coming home? We have business to discuss."

Her cheery yet firm acquisition causes my dick to rouse.

I shift to hide my growing erection and wait while Mason comes up with his answer. Once he tells her he'll clean up and be right here, she smiles wide, her face lighting up the whole room, and claps her hands.

"Great! I'm starving. Can we eat while we talk?" She asks as she steps away from the door and into the hallway.

My brow quirks up in question as I scramble to answer. "Um, sure. Lo Mein?"

"Ooo, yes! And egg rolls! Not spring rolls. Gross." She calls out over her shoulder.

"Taking a shower, Baby. Don't eat without me!"

And just like that, she disappears. Leaving me gaping after her with more questions than answers...

And one hell of a boner.

But, one thing's for sure... I'm not waiting another minute to cement our futures together. There's just too much that could go wrong, and all I have is so right.

40

~Chloe~

I take the most dreamy twenty-minute shower using the body wash that the guys bought for me. I've had a hell of a day but, given all the things that happened, I'm feeling light, happy, free.

Once I'm clean, I fold the towel around me and skip out to the closet, finding a new pair of leggings and a baggy, comfy-looking cold-shoulder sweatshirt.

Once I'm changed and I've brushed my hair and teeth, I wander back out into the hall.

Just as I step into the living room, the doorbell rings.

Gage startles me as he flies out of the kitchen, unlocks the front door, and pays the delivery man before kicking the door closed.

I was so enraptured by him that I missed Mason coming out of the kitchen. He steps in front of me, scoops me up, and twirls me around as he peppers my face with kisses and tells me about ten times how much he missed me.

Once I'm on my feet again, I look deep into his hazel eyes. "I love you, Mason."

His breathing stutters in his chest, and I watch his eyes widen in surprise. "I-I love you, too, Chloe." He responds before sweeping me back into his arms and kissing me senseless again.

"Food's ready!" Gage calls out from the kitchen, effectively breaking Mason and me out of our little happy bubble.

Wrapping my fingers with his, I pull Mason into the kitchen and sit down in front of a plate filled with at least four different dishes and another small plate with two egg rolls and some dumplings.

I giggle out, feeling lighter than I have in years, and they both look at me like I've lost it. "I'm sorry. I'm sorry." I say, gasping for breath between giggles. "But there's no way I can eat all of this." I snort a laugh and double over.

"Baby Girl...are you OK?" Gage asks, concern shining in his eyes.

I realize then that I probably look like a damn lunatic, so it's time to tell them what's going on.

"I... am great!" I exclaim, taking a big bite of an egg roll.

"Our paternity test came out positive, so I officially have an actual Dad. I have the best boyfriends a girl could ask for...and I didn't choke! I shot two scary-ass Russian douchebags, and I did it *without* you."

I smile to myself and chomp the end of a dumpling while truly feeling like the luckiest bitch alive. Then I remember...

"Oh, I also talked to Dad, and *I'm* not taking over. You two are."

I look down at my plate for stabbing a piece of orange chicken before plopping the whole thing in my mouth. The spicy, orange taste explodes on my tongue, and I moan out.

I half expect one of them to say something inappropriate but, neither of them do. Looking up, I notice that Mason has a fork full of food frozen in mid-air and Gage is frozen with his drink halfway to his mouth.

"What?" I ask, completely confused by their reaction. *Did I do something wrong?*

Gage takes a drink and clears his throat before leaning forward. "I- I'm sorry, Baby Girl. But what?" He asks, leaning in closer and furrowing his brows.

"Oh, I thought he told you the good news! So, yeah, I officially actually have a Dad! And maybe I'm being naive, but I feel like he really, genuinely has cared for me all these years. You know, in his own way. I mean, we have a long way to go but, this afternoon, when I called him, I said, 'Dad' and, I thought it would be weird but, at that moment, I felt like I needed *him*. Like a girl needing her Dad. And he didn't balk or freak out. Then when he got to the club, he embraced me and it was...I don't know. It was right. When he took me back to his house, he showed me the paternity test, and I can say now that I wouldn't have cared. He's been watching over me for years, and if that's not a real father, I don't know what is."

When I finish my rambling excitement, I pop another chicken in my mouth before gulping down some soda.

When I put my drink down, I realize neither of the men are moving...still.

"Um..." I trail off, my face firing up and my embarrassment taking over. "Do you not agree?" I ask, putting my fork down and feeling completely unsure about myself now.

"Oh, no, Angel. It's not that at all. It's...did you say we were taking over?" Mason asks incredulously.

My eyes go wide, and I wonder if they are going to be upset about it. "Um, well, yeah. I mean, we're going to train me in defense, shooting, all the things, but I can't run the Mafia. I don't want to. But, you two, you've proven yourselves time and time again. Including tonight. I told Dad how great you both were, how calm and ready for battle. How you made me feel safe, yet strong enough to be alone It was..." I struggle to find the right words without sounding like a groupie.

"It was fucking hot." I finally stated.

Silence envelopes us as they take in my word vomit.

I nervously pick through my lo mein, moving around the noodles instead of actually eating.

"Holy shit," Gage finally murmurs, huffing out a laugh.

Suddenly, Mason busts out laughing, clapping his hands wildly before clasping Gage on the shoulder. "So, do I call you Don in the bedroom now?" He jokes.

I chuckle along but see how Gage's eyes darken. "No, but Master would suffice."

Mason and I both go rigid as the levity of all the conversations comes barreling forward.

You...you want what?" I ask.

Gage coolly stands, swipes his hands down his shirt, and moves to stand between both of us.

Kneeling between us, he presents two small boxes. "I've uh, I've had these for a while. I just never imagined I would be able to use them. *Both* of them."

Looking at Mason, he takes his hand and flips open a small black box. In the middle is a black Tungsten ring with a blue inlay.

"Mason," He begins. "You were the first man I've ever given my heart to. And from the moment we first kissed, I knew I wanted you to be the only one. Will you marry me?"

Big, fat, crocodile tears stream down my face as Mason's mouth gapes open. The silence stretches until Mason falls to his knees, grabs Gage by his face, and kisses him hard.

"Yes, Master." He murmurs between kisses.

A sob rips from my throat at how amazingly beautiful these two men are, and I am so blessed to be part of this. It's exhilarating, wild, and utterly perfect.

When Mason releases Gage, Gage slips the ring on his finger and kisses him again before turning toward me.

Another sob hiccups from my chest, and I quickly wipe away my tears.

"Baby Girl, I have loved you from the first moment I laid eyes on you. I'll gladly fight anyone who tries to get in the way of that. Will you marry me and be ours forever?"

"Yes," I choke out between tears. "Yes, yes, yes!"

I lean down and kiss this man stupid before he can even get the ring out of the box. I lick his lips, demanding entrance, to which he happily obliges. He hums into my mouth, and I smile wide.

Once we break the kiss, we're both a sweaty, panting mess. My smile grows as his shaky hands bring the ring from the box and slides it onto my waiting finger.

A one-carat, square diamond sits in the middle of the ring. Each side of the ring alternates three blue diamonds with three clear diamonds.

It's perfect and stunning and so very Gage.

"I love you, Master," I say cheekily with a smile while wiping away more errant tears.

"I love you, too. Forever."

With a final kiss, he stands and makes his way back to the table, then shovels a huge mouthful of General Tso's into his mouth, happily humming as he does.

Mason and I look at each other, and his wide, infectious smile must mirror mine.

"I love you," I mouth.

"Love you, too." He responds, kissing my newly decorated hand.

41

~Epilogue~ Chloe

I'm standing in front of a full-length mirror, admiring my off-the-shoulder cream tulle maxi dress. The cream ombres down to a pink gradient around the skirt and makes me feel both beautiful and flirty.

My hair is slightly wavy and runs just past my shoulders. Other than my ring, I have a single pair of diamond stud earrings that my father picked for me.

It's been six months since the raid at Sky's the Limit, and six months since Gage proposed.

The door behind me swings open, and I see my father's shocked face in the mirror.

"Principessa, you look stunning." He says with a proud papa smile on his face.

"Thanks, Dad." I smile back.

I nervously run my hands down the front of my dress and check my makeup once more.

"Stop. There's nothing you can do to make yourself any more beautiful than you are every day. And, judging by how nervous those boys are out there, they feel the same."

He tilts his head and assesses me quietly. It used to freak me out, but now that we've spent so much time together, I know that it's just his way of choosing his words carefully and that he's just as nervous about messing this up as I am.

But we won't. Not after all the things we've been through and talked about.

"Thank you," I say, breaking the silence. "For, um, walking me down the aisle."

His stern look flashes into a wide smile as he holds out his elbow for me. Looping my arm through his, I lift up on my toes and press a light kiss to his cheek.

"Ready?" He asks.

"Ready!"

And my smile grows so wide it hurts.

As we walk out of the room and down the brightly lit chapel, the nerves begin to coil low in my belly.

"Should I tell them today?" I ask him with a low voice as we come to a stop in front of the door.

He chuckles under his breath and looks over at me. "What better way to celebrate your wedding?"

With a deep breath, I return his smile and nod in agreement.

Just then, the doors swing wide, and a very full chapel almost makes my knees buckle.

But, at the end of the aisle, in that very full chapel, are the two hottest, sweetest, most amazing men I've ever had the pleasure of knowing.

Jo, Tiffany, and a few others from Big and Beautiful are standing on the left side for me. It was a wild couple of weeks, but when I finally got around to explaining what I could explain, they forgave me, and we've stayed in touch ever since.

I am so lucky to have them here.

A bunch of Dad's men, I mean *Gage's* men, are scattered through the pews, and there are one or two at every available window and doorway.

Then, as we reach the front of the aisle, my eyes burn with tears. There's a seat wrapped in delicate lace with a picture of my mother sitting in the middle. I can't help it...a sob breaks out of me, and I feel Dad moving before a handkerchief appears through my blurred vision.

With a watery chuckle, I take the handkerchief and dab my eyes before officially reaching my two devastatingly handsome men.

They're both in crisp, black suits with cream shirts and a light pink pocket square that matches the pink in my dress.

"Angel," Mason coos with a huge smile, holding his hand out to me.

"Baby Girl," Gage calls, holding his hand out to me.

My smile is so wide that it physically hurts, but I refuse to stop.

"Treat my baby right," Dad says to the guys before kissing my cheek and walking to take his seat next to my mother's chair.

The guys guide me up the stairs, hand in hand, and we stand in front of the officiant.

As we say our vows, exchange words of love and hope, and forever, I realize that I truly am the luckiest girl in the world.

Gage was officially handed the reigns to run the family five months ago, and Dad is enjoying retirement.

The Russians have backed off after Gage and his men destroyed over a hundred Russian soldiers in three separate raids, and we announced our engagement right in the middle of the chaos.

Dad and I have a great relationship and we have family dinner every Sunday night. Which, of course, ends with talk of business since Gage and Mason are still getting used to leading and not being so, physically, involved.

And I have the best guys a girl could dream of, and I'm pregnant...with twins!

What can I say? I'm a lucky little bitch.

Acknowledgments

Thank you for joining Chloe as she rekindles her love in the place of
sin and salvation.
Shout out to Kayla and Em for beta reading, editing, and encouraging me not to scrap the whole project!
And of course, thank you, dear readers, for your continued support.
Don't forget to leave a review. :)

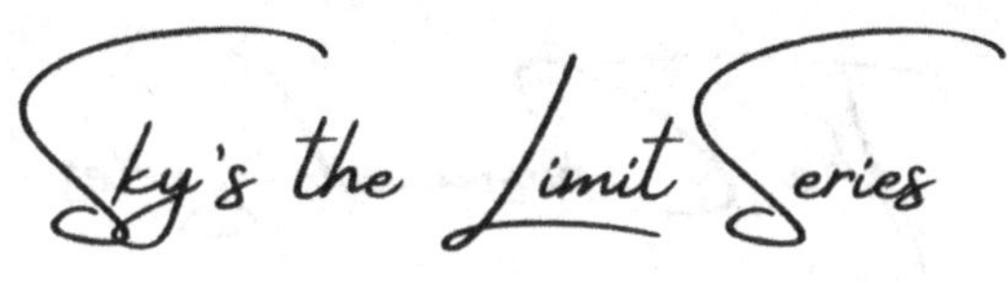

MENAGE OR REVERSE HAREM STANDALONES

Coveting Chloe
Mafia Menage

COMING SOON:

Daring Dahlia

Ensnaring Emma